THE MANOR AT PIRATE'S POINT

SKYLER ANHALT

The Manor at Pirate's Point © 2025 by Skyler Anhalt

Published by Rainbow Quartz Publishing

RQPublishing.com

RainbowQuartzPublishing@gmail.com

Edmonds, WA 98026

ISBN: 978-1-961714-90-8

Cover design by Miranda Townsend

Edited by Miranda Townsend

First Edition: April 2025

I would like to dedicate this book to my father. He isn't in the book, nor did he inspire the story. However, without him I would have never started rewriting this story. Thank you for believing in me.

CHAPTER I
NIGHTTIME WRECK

BAM! SLAM! The impact of my body against the wall knocked the breath from my lungs. Blood coated my tongue. Where am I?

I opened my eyes, squinting against the chaos around me. Was I on a boat? No, wait—a pirate ship. The sounds of crashing waves were all around.

A raging inferno consumed everything. The heat blistered my skin, the roar was deafening, and the acrid smell of burning filled the air.

What was happening?

Groggy and unsteady, I stumbled to my feet, the room swaying slightly. In a cracked mirror, I saw a reflection—a twisted, unfamiliar face staring back at me—but those weren't my own hollow eyes.

"Shipman, get over here!" shouted a deep voice.

The sudden, sharp sound of a man yelling made me whirl around. Or at least, I thought he was yelling at me. Around us, a fully crewed ship was in utter disarray. Men scattered along the deck, frantically trying to put out the roaring flames.

A relentless rain pelted my face, the drops like tiny, blunt daggers, each one a cool, heavy sting. The sky split open with a thunderous boom, sending a shiver down my spine. The fire, a hungry beast gnawing at the ship, cast an eerie, flickering glow on everything.

"Jack! Snap out of it, man," a crewman waved in my face.

"Jack?" I asked, glancing around in confusion.

"Get over here and help me with the ropes, or we'll be feeding the fish by dawn."

I focused on the man, his voice a raw, furious yell that cut through the air. A blond rat's nest crowned his head, his dark eyes glittered with barely suppressed fury, and a jagged scar, thick and angry, snaked down to reveal a weathered anchor tattoo on his neck.

"Oh... uh, okay," I stammered, stumbling forward.

Two steps, then a monstrous wave crashed over

the hull, sending me sprawling back onto the deck. I groaned, the world spinning around me. With a heave, I scrambled toward the fair-haired sailor, my feet losing their grip on the rain-slicked deck.

"What's gotten into you, Jack? It's like you've never sailed a day in your life," he snapped, shoving a rope into my hands.

"Sorry, must've hit my head," I mumbled, reaching up to feel my face—and freezing when I was met with a scruffy beard.

"You don't say," he said, shaking his head. Soaked through, his blue vest barely revealed the golden jackdaw emblem on his chest. His brown pants were frayed and too short, ending well above his ankles.

Instinctively, I tied a knot in the rope, my hands working faster than my mind. Sailing lessons when I was a kid came rushing back to me—muscle memory, I guessed.

"Jack!" the crewman shouted again.

"Huh?" I blinked at him, dazed.

"Snap out of it!"

BAM

Another boom echoed, jolting me.

A sudden, violent lurch, sent me stumbling backward. "What was that?"

"Nothing good," a raspy voice answered grimly from somewhere behind me.

The horrifying command, "ABANDON SHIP!" echoed across the deck.

A cold, salty spray engulfed me as I was tossed backward, my body hitting the slick guardrail with a sickening crunch. Pain exploded in my ribs, and I couldn't breathe. Gasping for air, I pushed myself to my feet just as the ship tilted dangerously.

A second powerful wave hit, and suddenly I was thrown sideways. The cold, salty water engulfed me, my body hitting the slick guardrail again with a sickening crunch. Pain exploded in my ribs, and my lungs seized. Fighting for breath, I grasped desperately at the rail, but my grip failed.

The world spun as I was hurled overboard into the sea, swallowed by darkness.

CHAPTER 2
WELCOME TO MY LIFE

B*eep! Beep! Beep!* "Damn, it's three a.m. already," I groaned, silencing the insistent alarm's jarring shriek and wishing for just a few more hours of sleep. "What a crazy dream."

My name is James Shipman, and I spent nine years of my childhood in foster care. The concrete walls of my basement room were icy to the touch, and a persistent, earthy smell of mildew permeated the stale air. I climbed out of bed—or what passed for a bed, anyway. It was an old army cot that creaked every time I shifted.

Three years ago, Pam and Derrick Goodman adopted me, and though they provided me with this damp hellhole, it's a constant reminder of my wish that they hadn't. It's not like they wanted me for anything other than free labor. They had a spare bedroom upstairs, but I was "too filthy for the public" to sleep somewhere decent.

Their words, not mine.

I pulled on a threadbare hoodie and headed upstairs, careful to step lightly on the old wooden steps. Derrick hated being woken up early, and Pam... well, she just hated me.

The kitchen was a disaster, as usual: plates piled high in the sink, crumbs scattered across the counters, and a sticky puddle of something I didn't want to identify congealing near the fridge.

I sighed. Might as well get started.

I was up to my elbows in soap suds when I heard them—heavy footsteps thudding on the stairs: Derrick. And the faint shuffle of slippers dragging across the floor: Pam.

My heart skipped a beat.

I kept my head down, scrubbing furiously at a frying pan, hoping they wouldn't notice me. Derrick stumbled into the kitchen first, his breath reeking of whiskey even from across the room. His shirt was wrinkled, and his belt hung loosely at his waist. Derrick scratched his belly and grunted something unintelligible.

With hollow eyes, Pam followed him, her gaze

moving across the room in a mechanical scan that failed to register any details. She was a shell of whoever she used to be, with tangled, dirty-blonde hair that she'd given up trying to tame. Her pharmacy job paid well, but most of her paycheck went to the pills she stole and popped like candy.

They didn't say anything to me—not today, anyway. Derrick grabbed a half-empty beer can off the counter and guzzled it down in one go, belching loudly before lumbering back toward the living room. Pam rifled through her purse, muttering under her breath until she found what she was looking for—a little orange bottle. She twisted the cap off with trembling fingers and swallowed two pills dry.

I glanced over my shoulder, just to make sure they were both occupied, and breathed a quiet sigh of relief.

They'd been like this for years now. I was hopeful at first—when they adopted me, they seemed normal enough. But it didn't take long for their masks to slip. Derrick's temper flared the first time I spilled milk on the counter, and Pam started retreating into her pill bottles soon after.

Now, Derrick hit me just because he could. He said he was "teaching me a lesson," but I knew better. And Pam? She didn't hit me, but her words cut deeper than his fists ever could.

"You're useless."

"Pathetic."

"No wonder no one wanted you."

Sometimes, I thought I'd rather take the punches. At least bruises fade.

I finished the dishes and started tying up the trash bag when there was a knock at the door. My stomach dropped.

"Go downstairs," Pam hissed at me, suddenly alert.

I didn't argue. I knew the drill. With the trash bag in tow, I went to the basement, leaving the door open a crack so I could listen.

"Hello!" a cheerful voice greeted Pam. It was Mrs. Chapman from next door, her apron dusted with flour, the telltale aroma of baking cookies clinging to her, ready for a friendly chat.

"Pam! Derrick! I brought some extra snickerdoodles for you and your son."

"Oh, thank you!" Pam gushed, her tone sickly sweet. "But James isn't here right now. He's off playing with his friends; you know how boys his age are."

I clenched my fists. Friends? Really?

Upstairs, Pam laughed lightly, as though she didn't have a care in the world. The sound made my skin crawl. I slumped onto my cot, listening to the muffled conversation as Mrs. Chapman prattled on about her garden and the upcoming neighborhood barbecue.

When the front door finally closed, I climbed back upstairs and tossed the trash bag out onto the curb. No cookies for me, of course—not that I expected any.

Trudging down the street, I braced myself for another long day at school. Just another hellhole to survive.

CHAPTER 3
MY SCHOOL SUCKS

The metallic clang of a locker door slamming echoed down the brightly lit, overly crowded hallway as I stepped into the chaotic scene that was high school.

There, in the middle of the crowd, stood my best friend, Tom O'Hara, squinting at the world through his smudged glasses and wearing his signature too-big pants, cinched awkwardly at the waist. His green T-shirt, faded in places from many washes, read: "Want to hear a joke about potassium? K." Of course, the first time he wore it, he grinned like he'd just told the best joke in the world.

"Hey, what's up, Tom?" I called out, weaving through the sea of students to meet him.

Tom grinned, though it looked a bit strained.

"Not much, just trying to avoid Alex Peabody," he sighed.

"Yeah, that tracks. He sucks," I said, shaking my head.

"Well, at least we don't have him in first period," Tom said, his words laced with fake optimism.

"True. Come on, let's get to class before we're late," I said, nudging him in the arm.

A sudden breeze wove its way through the crowd of students and pushed me forward. A faint whisper, carried on the wind, sent a shiver down my spine. It seemed to say, "it's almost time to return..." The chilling words left me stunned. I quickly glanced around to see how my classmates reacted to this strange wind. No one seemed affected. Kids shuffled through the halls, business as usual.

"Did you hear that?" I asked Tom.

Tom looked back at me with a curiously arched brow. "Hear what?"

"Hmm, never mind," I said, following him into class.

The school was nothing to brag about. The hallways reeked of sweat and stale air, a permanent stench that lingered no matter how many air fresheners the janitors tried to hide in the corners. Both the classroom doors and the lockers were identical in color—though the metal frames of the doors showed more wear from years of abuse. The walls were mostly white, except for the occasional mystery stain that the school clearly couldn't afford to clean.

Students crowded the hallways, shouting and shoving as they rushed to their next classes. They ignored the teachers and treated the rules as mere suggestions. Authority held little sway here.

Tom and I slipped into Algebra, taking our usual seats near the back. Our teacher shuffled in shortly after, looking like he hadn't slept in weeks. He was a middle-aged man with a scruffy beard, baggy eyes, and a perpetually slouched posture. He wore a wrinkled, misbuttoned pink button-up shirt, and his black pants hung limply off his frame.

"Good morning, class," he mumbled, his voice devoid of energy. "Please take your seats quietly and turn to page twenty-six in your math books."

The math book was one of the few decent things in the school—a blue hardcover with gold lettering that proudly announced algebra. It was probably the nicest book we'd see all year.

The class wasn't hard. Most days, we finished the lesson with time to spare. As the teacher droned on about solving equations, I leaned over to Tom.

"Hey, guess what?" I whispered, my voice tinged with excitement.

"What?" Tom looked up from his notes with mild curiosity.

"I had the craziest dream last night," I said. "I was on this pirate ship during a storm. It was sinking, and everyone kept calling me Jack. I didn't even look like myself."

Tom furrowed his brow. "That's... weird."

"Right? And it gets stranger," I continued. "The ship was going down, and I got flung into a life raft or something. I woke up right after that, but my ribs hurt—like, in the exact same spot I got hit in the dream."

Tom looked at me, his expression somewhere between intrigued and concerned. "That's really weird," he said slowly, a thoughtful silence hanging in the air as he considered my words.

Before I could respond, the bell rang, signaling the end of first period.

The hallway was a jumble of voices and slamming lockers. I glanced back at Tom to say something, but before I could get the words out, I crashed into someone, the sudden contact jolting me.

"Sorry!" I blurted out, spinning around to face whoever I'd bumped into.

The voice that answered back was raspy, like dry leaves skittering across pavement. "Well, if it isn't the two orphan rats."

Great.

It was Alex Peabody.

CHAPTER 4
SCHOOL FIGHT

My body slammed against the unforgiving floor, a sharp pain shooting through me. My jaw throbbed, a dull ache spreading across my face as I felt the warm trickle of blood down my chin.

"Damn," I muttered under my breath. Apparently, I'd upset Alex when I bumped into him, and now I was receiving what he called "punishment." This typically consisted of a black eye, a couple of bruised ribs, and maybe some internal bleeding that would fade in a few hours.

Luckily, it didn't get out of hand this time.

Alex pulled his arm back to deliver another blow before Tom burst in, grabbing Alex's arm in time. "Don't you lay a hand on mas—James."

A deep, commanding voice cut through the chaos of the hallway. "What's going on here?"

The sound froze me in place. I glanced back, and there he was—Mr. Smith, our principal, his eyes narrowed, looking severe and imposing.

"Oh, Mr. Smith. I'm sorry about this," I said quickly, shuffling to the side instinctively.

Mr. Smith was a terrifying figure. Standing at six feet four inches, with dark, curly black hair and a glare that could make even the toughest Green Beret tremble, he wasn't someone you wanted to cross.

His gaze felt heavy, a cold weight pressing down on me as Mr. Smith stared right through me. "My office. After school. Detention," he said with cold, clipped words.

"Yes, Mr. Smith," Alex and I replied in unison, neither of us daring to argue.

Not exactly the ideal start to the day, but I'd had worse.

By some miracle, I made it to my second-period class without any more trouble. Tom and I shared all the same classes—we'd planned it that way when we signed up for courses. It was one of the few things that made school tolerable.

Our second period was history, and as we settled

into our seats, our teacher, Mr. Clark, greeted us with his usual enthusiasm.

"Take out your textbooks and turn to page 189," he said, clapping his hands together as he reached the front of the room. "Today, we'll be learning about some of the history of our little town."

Mr. Clark was one of the few teachers I actually liked. He was polite, energetic, and genuinely seemed to enjoy teaching. His ruffled brown hair always looked like he'd just rolled out of bed, and his white button-up shirt had a faint coffee stain near the collar that no amount of scrubbing had removed.

When he wasn't teaching, you could usually find him in the library, sipping coffee and losing himself in a fantasy novel. Get him talking about one of his favorites or a piece of obscure history, and he'd happily go on for hours.

He approached the lesson with his characteristic vigor. He leaned forward, voice dropping to a conspiratorial whisper. "Way back in the 1830s and 1840s, there was actually quite a bit of pirate activity in this region."

The word "pirate" jolted me back to Mr. Clark's lesson. I could almost smell the salty spray of the ocean.

"One of the most infamous pirates in this area was a strong and cunning captain named Jack Shipman," Mr. Clark said with a grin.

I blinked.

Shipman?

Jack Shipman?!

CHAPTER 5

PUNISHMENT

SMASH!

Alex shoved me against the cold metal lockers as we entered Mr. Smith's office, the noise rattling loudly.

The principal, needless to say, wasn't looking.

Alex and I found ourselves the focus of Mr. Smith's icy glare. "You two boys," he stated, his tone sharp and unrelenting, "have quite a bit of explaining to do."

"Well, you see, it was an accident, Mr. Smith," I stammered, my voice barely louder than a whisper. "I bumped into Alex by accident."

Mr. Smith raised an eyebrow, unimpressed. "Oh?"

That one word, spoken in his deep, gravelly voice, sent a chill down my spine.

"So, it was an accident that Alex punched you?" he asked, his tone sharp and skeptical.

"No," I admitted reluctantly, clenching my fists at my sides.

"I think you're covering for him. But why?" Mr. Smith leaned in close, his eyes narrowing.

"I-I would never..." I stammered, sweat trickling down my temple.

"Well, if that's the truth, then you two can sit here for the hour under the camera's supervision," he said, straightening up and walking toward the door.

His hand rested on the knob for a moment as he glanced back. "See you boys tomorrow."

The door clicked shut behind him, leaving Alex and me in tense silence.

The fight replayed in my mind, and I kept circling back to Tom. What was he doing in the hallway? How was he so strong? Most people can't stop a punch mid-swing. I never would have guessed Tom was capable of that.

Springfield Park is where I first met Tom. I ran into him one morning while going to school. I wasn't paying much attention, just walking past like I always did, when out of nowhere, this kid sprinted up to me, talking a mile a minute. From what little I grasped, he was talking about space-time paradoxes and the theoretical possibility of teleportation.

At first, I thought he was annoying. And weird. His T-shirt had some nerdy science joke on it, his hair was a mess, and he had this wild energy, like he existed on a completely different frequency. Not that I had any room to judge.

But somehow, despite the chaotic first impression, we ended up walking together. And talking.

A lot.

It was like we had the same brain, wired in the same way, tuned into the same unspoken wavelength. He just got me, in a way most people didn't.

When we reached the school, he stopped at the edge of the sidewalk. I hesitated, not wanting the conversation to end. "So... how do we hang out again?" I asked.

Tom just grinned. "Don't worry. We'll meet again... soon."

The very next day, he transferred into my school. And from that moment on, we've been inseparable.

Only today did the strangeness of that truly sink

in. Also, he never talks about his family or where he lives. Thinking about it, Tom's been with me the whole time, yet despite his kindness, loyalty, and humor, I know almost nothing personal about him.

Does he have siblings? I don't know.

What are his parents' names? I don't know.

I was going to have to be a better friend to Tom and ask him more questions about his life.

Later that evening, under the weak light of the setting sun, I paid for the detention in blood, each wound a searing reminder. Derrick's fist slammed into my jaw, sending another spray of blood onto the floor.

"You ungrateful little..." he cut himself off. "Why couldn't you just be normal and stay out of trouble?" he bellowed, his whiskey-soaked breath assaulting my nose.

Another punch landed—this time in my stomach. My knees buckled, and I crumpled to the ground, clutching my ribs and gasping for air. The pain was searing, as if someone had lit a fire inside my chest.

"Now look what you've done!" Derrick roared. "You spilled blood on our floor! Clean it up!"

Another punch, and my vision went dark.

I woke up soaked in a pool of my own blood.

Pain radiated from my ribs with every shallow breath. Tears stung my eyes, and my body trembled uncontrollably.

"Get up," Pam barked, hauling me to my feet.

I bit back a scream as my ribs shifted under her grip, sending a bolt of agony through my torso. That's when I realized— it felt like Derrick had broken one of my ribs.

Pam thrust a bucket of soapy water into my hands. "Clean up your mess and go back to the basement. I don't want to see your face for the rest of the night. Derrick will bring down the scraps later."

"Yes, ma'am," I muttered, my voice hollow.

The floor seemed endless as I scrubbed, each movement a fresh wave of pain from my chest. I quickly learned that shallow breaths hurt less, and I clung to that small relief as I worked.

It took an hour, maybe longer, but eventually, the bloodstains were gone. The throbbing in my head and the sharp stabs of pain in my ribs made each step a monumental effort on my way back to the damp, dark basement.

Sometime around nine, Derrick opened the door and tossed down my "dinner."

A box hit the ground, and a pile of scraps clattered onto the floor—barely enough to call food. I sorted through the box, finding a small piece of steak on a bone, a half-eaten, shriveled pile of broccoli, and the crust of a stale piece of bread.

I ate what I could, swallowing around the lump in my throat, knowing this was all I'd get for the night. When the meal was gone, I lay down on the old army cot, careful not to aggravate my ribs, and closed my eyes.

The pain didn't fade, but exhaustion eventually pulled me under.

CHAPTER 6
BACK ON THE SEA

T he icy water shocked me awake, splashing onto my face and sending shivers down my spine.

I opened my eyes to a golden sunrise stretching across clear skies, broken only by a few scattered clouds.

Slowly, I came to my senses, the ache in my body a painful reminder of being tossed overboard. I turned my head, and there it was—the ship, half-submerged in the water. What remained of it still smoldered, thin tendrils of smoke rising into the morning air.

The water around me shimmered with an unsettling red tint. A body floated by, face down, the familiar vest confirming who it was. My chest tightened. It was the crewman from last night.

I reached out, wincing as every movement sent a sharp pain through my ribs, and hauled him onto the raft. His body lay unflinching, cold to the touch, the skin already taking on a bluish pallor. Despite knowing the answer, I meticulously checked for any signs of life; not a breath, not a heartbeat, not a sound.

Suddenly, grief hit me like waves crashing against jagged rocks. A memory flashed through my mind—me and the crewman, laughing, drinking, playing blackjack at a worn wooden table. His name was Nathan.

But how did I...? A sudden flood of memories, not my own, filled my mind.

I closed his eyes gently and removed his vest. "With this vest, your memory will live on in my family forever," I whispered, my voice barely audible. Then, with a heavy heart, I set him back into the water, watching as he floated away.

I forced myself to stand, scanning the horizon. Clear seas in every direction, but no sign of help. I sank back down, my mind racing. What was I supposed to do now, the weight of the world heavy on my shoulders and the path ahead unclear?

After a moment, I stretched and looked more carefully. This time, I saw it—a small island in the distance. Relief flooded through me. Grabbing the compass attached to my hip, I found the island lay to the north.

But then reality set in. I had no paddles.

Panic bubbled up as I searched the dinghy. There was nothing useful, just an old rope coiled and tucked away. Securing one end of the rope to the raft, I wrapped the other end tightly around my waist, feeling the rough hemp against my skin. Taking a deep breath, I plunged into the sea.

The saltwater stung my skin as I swam toward the wreckage. The half-intact ladder built into the side of the hull offered a way up. I climbed it carefully, each rung groaning under my weight, until I reached the deck.

Untying the rope from my waist, I secured it to a sturdy piece of railing and began pulling the raft closer to the ship. It was slow, exhausting work, but eventually, I got the raft within reach.

Standing on the scorched deck, I took in the ruins of the ship. The main mast had been burned through, lying shattered off the starboard side. Chunks of the hull were blasted away, leaving jagged holes where cannonballs had struck. What little remained intact was charred, splintered, and waterlogged.

I moved carefully, searching for anything of value. Most of the treasure was gone, but I managed to find some food, a few barrels of fresh water, and —thankfully—a pair of oars. I placed them next to the raft and stretched, my muscles screaming in protest with each movement.

That's when my eyes landed on the captain's cabin.

The door hung slightly open, a jagged hole where the lock used to be. The captain, a stern figure with eyes like flint, never allowed anyone past the threshold. But curiosity got the better of me.

I pushed the door open and stepped inside.

The storm had left its mark on the once orderly cabin, with the aftermath reflecting the turbulent emotions that had likely accompanied it. The crooked paintings mirrored the sense of disorientation and imbalance that had swept through the room, while the scattered tools and instruments spoke to a sense of upheaval and chaos. Jumbled and out of place, the fine wood of the furniture seemed to groan under the weight of loss permeating the space. The detailed map, once a symbol of direction and purpose, now lay in disarray, mirroring the confusion and uncertainty that had taken hold. The once serene cabin had turned into a tumultuous battleground of emotions.

I approached the map, staring at it in awe. Every line was precise, every landmark detailed. Even the sea routes had been meticulously charted.

Carefully, I unpinned it, rolled it up, and stashed it in a cloth bag I found nearby. This was too valuable to leave behind.

I took one last look at the cabin, then gathered the supplies and loaded them onto the raft.

As I climbed down the ladder, my foot slipped.

The last rung gave way with a loud CRACK, and I tumbled backward into the wooden raft. My body slammed into the side of the ship, pain exploding across every inch of me.

The world spun as I lay there, gasping for breath.

CHAPTER 7

DAY AT THE ORPHANAGE

The alarm clock blared its usual obnoxious tune, but for once, I didn't mind. I woke up early, excited. Today was going to be different.

I rushed through my chores, moving with a speed that surprised even me. Dishes? Done. Trash? Out. Floors? Sparkling. By the time I was finished, the house was still silent—Pam and Derrick were sound asleep.

Perfect.

Grabbing a piece of paper, I scribbled out a note:

Left for school early. I finished the chores. Be back after school.

Except I wasn't going to school.

With a grin plastered across my face, I slipped

out the door and headed in the opposite direction—toward Meadowview Haven, the orphanage where I grew up. I had plenty of questions, and I needed some answers.

The Goodman house disappeared behind me as I walked briskly toward Meadowview. My heart felt lighter with every step. I hadn't been back in so long, and the thought of seeing everyone again filled me with a warmth I hadn't felt in years.

As much as I wished I could go to the police and tell them about the terrible things that happened at the Goodmans' house, I couldn't trust them either. As chief of police, Pam's father always had a hard, skeptical look in his eyes. He wasn't about to trust a word from their "troubled" adopted child. Plus, I'd promised Maggie, the old caregiver at Meadowview, that once I got adopted, I would stick it out. No matter what.

When I finally arrived, the sight took my breath away. The silver gateway to Meadowview stood tall and proud, its intricate design depicting a meadow woven through a lush forest. Beyond it, kids played joyously on the freshly cut lawn in front of the grand brick building.

Meadowview itself was as beautiful as I remembered. The old brick walls were adorned with carefully maintained vines, and its towering structure resembled a chapel, complete with extraordinary stained-glass windows. The garden beds out front were alive with bright flowers and vegetables, a testament to the caretakers' dedication.

"James!"

I turned just in time to see Lucy Casa running toward me, her blonde hair bouncing as she sprinted across the lawn.

"Hey, Lucy!" I said, kneeling down as she barreled into me with a joyful hug. I winced at the pain of being touched. I didn't feel as bad as yesterday, but everything still hurt today.

"It's been so long, James. Guys, come look!" she called to the other kids, her brown eyes shining with excitement.

Timothy and Bella appeared moments later, their faces lighting up at the sight of me.

Lucy was nine now, her medium-length hair messy from running around. She was small for her age, but her big personality more than made up for it. Bella, a tomboy through and through, stood a little taller with her short black hair looking as wild as ever. She was ten and always had a knack for disappearing into town, only to return at sunset as if nothing happened.

And then there was Tim. He was twelve now, taller than I remembered, with short, well-kept black hair and an air of calm authority. Tim had always been like my second-in-command, the one who looked out for everyone else. When I left, I told him to keep the group safe, and he'd taken the responsibility seriously.

"Hey, big bro! What's life like outside, in your new home?" Tim asked, his voice brimming with excitement.

I hesitated, the weight of my situation settling on my shoulders. "It's... great," I lied, forcing a smile. "The new foster parents are treating me really well, and school is amazing."

It felt wrong to lie, but what else could I do? They didn't need to know the truth. Not now.

"Oh, cool!" the kids chimed in unison, their excitement washing away my guilt—at least for the moment.

"Hey, James, you should go see Miss Mary," Tim said, his voice calm and steady. "She's been wondering about how you've been doing. I think she's been worried."

His words caught me off guard. He knew. And if he knew, that meant Mary did, too.

I smiled warmly at Tim, trying to mask my

unease. "Wow, look how much you've grown," I said, ruffling his hair.

I saw tears welling up in his eyes, but he blinked them away quickly. Not wanting to upset the younger kids, I stood up and said gently, "Hey, Tim, why don't you take Lucy and Bella to check on the plants? They look thirsty."

Tim nodded, his voice steady. "Yeah, come on, guys. Let's do as James says." He gave me a small smile before leading the others toward the garden.

"Miss Mary, it's been a while," I said as I stepped into her office.

The room hadn't changed—pictures of the kids, past and present, covered the walls. Each frame told a story, a memory preserved in time.

"Good to see you, James," Mary said, her tone cool and measured. "How are you?"

"I'm doing great," I said, mustering every bit of believability into the words that I could.

Her piercing gaze told me everything I needed to know. She wasn't buying my act.

I shifted uncomfortably as she stared me down. "How have you been?"

"I'm fine. But how are you really, James?" she asked, her voice soft but firm.

Before I could answer, she cut me off. "Actually,

I'll save you the trouble. I heard through the grapevine about your situation. And even if I hadn't, it's obvious just looking at you—you're covered in wounds, fresh bruises, and you're limping!"

Her words hit like a punch.

"It's really not that bad. You don't have to worry, I promise," I said, taking a step back and sighing.

"It's not okay, James," she snapped, her voice rising with frustration before she exhaled sharply, trying to calm herself.

"I'm fine, really," and I didn't lie. I would be fine as long as I kept my head down.

Miss Mary hesitated, then sat down on the edge of the desk, folding her hands in her lap. "James, do you know how you came to be here at the orphanage?"

I shifted uncomfortably. "I know my parents died in a car crash."

She nodded. "That's right. But there's more to it than that."

I blinked. More? My stomach twisted as she continued.

"When you were found, you were wandering the streets alone. A woman, an older lady, saw you and realized something was wrong. She took you to the authorities, and that's how you ended up here."

35

I frowned. "I was just... walking around?"

"Yes. The woman who found you had no idea you were connected to the crash. No one did. Not at first. But when the police started searching for your family, they realized you were the missing child from the accident. They did everything they could to find someone-anyone-to take you in, but no relatives came forward."

I swallowed hard. It made sense in a way. I had always known my parents were gone. But to hear that I had been out there, alone, wandering... it made my skin prickle.

Miss Mary reached out and placed a gentle hand on my shoulder. "James, I promise you, they didn't give up easily."

I nodded slowly, my mind spinning. So that was it. Some stranger had found me. Brought me here. And the world had just... moved on.

Miss Mary's lips pressed into a thin line, but she didn't argue. Instead, she reached for a folded piece of paper on her desk and handed it to me.

CHAPTER 8
THE MANOR AT PIRATE'S POINT

My heart hammered against my ribs, a frantic drumbeat, as I carefully unfolded the paper Miss Mary gave me; it felt strangely stiff and cool to the touch.

"My grandpa was rich?" I whispered, my voice tinged with disbelief.

"Not exactly. Your great-grandpa was," Miss Mary said, her tone calm as she glanced over her shoulder to ensure the other kids didn't hear. "He owned a manor at the top of the nearby point."

"A manor?" I asked, trying to keep my excitement in check. My mind raced with possibilities. Could this be my chance to finally escape the suffocating control of the Goodmans and breathe freely again?

"Yes," she said, lowering her voice even further. "And if the rumors are true, your family's butlers still live there. Here." She unfolded the map, smoothing it out on the desk before handing it to me. "This shows the way to the manor. If you decide to go, this will help you find it."

"I don't understand," I said.

"I know this is a lot to take in," she breathed. "I wanted to make sure before I told you anything."

"How did you find this?" I asked. Tears welled in my eyes.

Miss Mary rubbed her hands together like she was trying to warm them up. "I've spent the last three years digging through archives, records, anything I could get my hands on," she admitted. "There wasn't a lot of information readily available, but I kept looking."

I stared at her. "The whole time?"

She nodded. "It wasn't easy. A lot of the records were lost, misplaced, or... well, like someone wanted them gone. I found traces—mentions of your great-grandfather's estate, old property filings, and... this." She tapped the map.

I swallowed hard, my fingers curling around the paper. It was thick, the edges frayed like it had been folded and unfolded a thousand times.

"Why?" My voice cracked. "Why go through all that trouble?"

She gave me a small, sad smile. "Because you deserved better. I always knew something felt off with the Goodmans. You've suffered enough."

"Thank you," I said, clutching the map tightly. Worry crept into my voice as I glanced at the clock. "I should go, though. If I'm late... let's just say, it won't be good."

"You'd better get going, then," Miss Mary said, offering a kind smile. "The kids seem busy, so I'll tell them you said goodbye."

"Thanks. I'll try to stop by again soon," I said, walking toward the large, engraved wooden door.

A harsh, angry voice cut through the silence the moment I opened the Goodmans' front door.

"Where were you?" Derrick's bellow echoed through the room, a venomous sound thick with rage.

I froze in place as he stormed toward me, his face red and his fists clenched. "You weren't at school. I know that. So where were you?"

"I was... at school," I stammered.

"Don't lie to me, boy," he roared, spit flying with each word. "No, not boy. You're a thing. A wretched little thing, only good for doing our work!"

The raw fury in his voice was a physical force, making my knees buckle.

"What makes you think I'm lying?" I asked, my confidence crumbling with each passing second.

He paused for a moment, his tone dropping to something almost calm, which somehow made it worse. "We got a call from your school. They told us you weren't there today."

Panic surged through me. The attendance call. I'd forgotten all about it.

Before I could respond, Derrick grabbed me by the arm and threw me against the wall. His anger was unlike anything I'd seen before. He shoved me through the house, slamming me into anything in his path—furniture, walls, even the sharp corner of the kitchen counter.

"You think you can lie to me?!" he screamed. His words blurred as his rage boiled over.

He grabbed a fistful of my hair, yanking me upright, and slammed my head into the glass coffee table. The sound of shattering glass filled my ears, a brutal cacophony that was accompanied by the immediate, intense pain of a jagged shard against my skin.

Blood poured from the cuts, dripping onto the

floor. The sight of it seemed to snap Derrick out of his frenzy. For a brief moment, he panicked, grabbing a rag to press against my face in an attempt to stop the bleeding. But his concern wasn't for me—it was for the mess I was making.

When it was over, I was left to clean up the disaster. Blood, shattered glass, overturned furniture—it felt like the entire house was a war zone, and I was the only one tasked with putting it back together.

The pain was excruciating, and my vision blurred several times as I tried to stay upright. Each breath sent a searing pain through my cracked ribs, while every flinch made the cuts on my face burn. By the time I was done, I could barely stand.

I stumbled down to the basement, grateful to finally collapse onto my cot. Sometime later, Derrick tossed down the scraps he called dinner.

I picked through the pile, finding a few small edible bits of bread and meat. As I ate, my mind drifted back to what Miss Mary had said.

Next chance you get, I think you should go. Here is a map of the area when or if you decide to make your way over to your family manor...

I unfolded the map, staring at the path it

outlined. I can't tell how far it is, but it doesn't seem close. Nothing could deter me though. Perhaps leaving would be sooner than I thought.

CHAPTER 9
PREPARATION

The jingle of loose change in my pocket was a rhythmic counterpoint to my hurried steps down the busy street, each clink a small comfort as I plotted my next move. After last night, I'd made up my mind—I was going to my family's old manor. But first, I needed supplies. Food was obvious, but I couldn't take any from the Goodmans. They kept track of everything, and the second something went missing, they'd know.

Asking Tom for help was out of the question. He'd be suspicious, and I wasn't ready to explain. That left only one option, a desperate, shameful one: stealing.

Not from a big store, though. Too many cameras, too many employees. I needed somewhere small, somewhere easy to slip in and out unnoticed. Then I remembered a girl in class talking about her new job at a small convenience store. It didn't have cameras, and it wasn't busy. Perfect.

The store was small, the kind of place where the air smelled faintly of stale chips and floor cleaner. My eyes scanned the shelves, trying to look casual, even though my heart raced.

I needed food, water, and, if I could find one, a survival book. My plan was simple—grab what I needed, buy something small like gum to seem less suspicious, and get out.

I grabbed a few items quickly, stuffing them into my backpack: a water bottle, granola bars, a pack of Skittles, and a book called Survival Skills for Beginners. I turned the corner, picked out a pack of gum, and walked up to the counter, trying to calm my nerves.

The cashier didn't look thrilled to be there. Her blonde hair was slightly tangled, and her baby-blue uniform was wrinkled and creased. She looked at me with tired eyes, barely lifting her head.

"Excuse me, Miss. I'd like to purchase this pack of gum," I said.

She raised an eyebrow, clearly unimpressed. "Kid, you don't need to be so formal. Hand it over."

"Sorry, Miss. Here." I slid the gum onto the counter.

She scanned it lazily. "A dollar thirty-five," she said, holding out her hand.

I handed her two dollars, trying not to look as nervous as I felt.

"Have a good day, kid," she muttered, slouching back over the counter.

"Uh, yes. You too, Miss," I said, stiff as a board.

"Scram, kid," she barked, making me jump.

I didn't stick around. Clutching my backpack, I rushed out of the store and down the street, my heart pounding in my ears.

That night, back in the basement, I emptied the contents of my backpack onto my cot. It wasn't much.

I sighed, flipping open the book and scanning the index. "Foods in the woods, page 123." I flipped to the page.

"The wild huckleberry is a very common source of food for someone without extensive knowledge of the woods. Its bright red berries and roundish leaves make it stand out, as shown in the picture on the left..."

I stared at the image, committing it to memory. It wasn't much, but it was a start.

With this, I had everything I needed. Tomorrow, I would leave for the manor.

CHAPTER 10
NIGHT IN THE WOODS

The sound of the city bus brakes jolted me out of my thoughts as it slowed to the curb.

Miss Mary had carefully marked the map with the bus stop location and schedule, so I knew exactly where to be this morning. Leaving the house early, I'd walked briskly to the station. I was hoping no one would notice I was gone before I could get far enough away.

The city bus was free for anyone under eighteen, so I didn't need to worry about money. When it arrived, I climbed aboard, noticing that only a handful of people were on at this hour. They all looked tired, irritated, or maybe even drunk—definitely not the lively crowd I'd hoped for.

It felt like forever before the bus finally reached the bottom of a steep hill described in my map.

The forest that covered the hillside was alive. Birds of every kind chirped harmoniously, their songs creating a small orchestra that seemed to welcome me. Trees creaked in rhythm, their trunks swaying gently as the wind rustled the leaves above. It was like watching siblings playing an endless game, chasing one another through the shadows and sunlight that danced across the forest floor.

Everything about the place felt vibrant, almost magical.

As I made my way up the side of this mountain —it was too big to be a simple hill—I couldn't help but marvel at the surrounding beauty. The further I walked, the more the sunlight seemed to intensify, filtering through the trees until it formed a blinding wall of light ahead. Shielding my eyes, I pushed through.

On the other side of the trees was a meadow, a breathtaking expanse of wildflowers and tall grasses that made me stop in my tracks. The green stretched as far as I could see. Bugs buzzed lazily, adding an air of life and energy.

I lay down in the soft grass, amazed at how comfortable it felt, and let the warmth of the sun wash over me. Before I knew it, I'd drifted off to sleep.

When I woke up, the sun was much lower in the sky. The meadow, once full of buzzing life, was quieter now. Even the forest critters seemed to settle in for the evening.

While the meadow was worth the nap, I'd hoped to get a little further. So, I got up and continued walking.

The forest grew darker as time passed, but then I stumbled upon a lively creek. The water was crystal clear, the smooth, round stones at the bottom gleaming like polished gems. Sunlight filtered through the trees, bouncing off the water and casting warm, golden reflections all around.

I followed the creek until I came across an old, half-collapsed stone building. One wall was completely gone, and the wooden roof had caved in long ago.

"THIS MIGHT BE A GOOD SPOT TO CATCH MY BREATH," I said, glancing around. I dropped my bag and sat down cross-legged, already feeling my stomach grumble.

"Okay, food," I muttered. I reached into my bag

and pulled out the survival book I'd grabbed from the store. The pages crinkled as I flipped through them. "Fire... shelter... ah, here—food."

My finger stopped on a page titled *Edible Plants and Foraging Basics*. "Many wild berries are edible and packed with nutrients. Look for clusters growing on bushes in sunny areas. Common examples include blackberries, salmonberries, and—huckleberries."

"Huckleberries," I repeated. "Didn't I see some of those back near that old trail?"

I shoved the book back into my bag and stood up, brushing off my jeans. The sun was starting to drop behind the trees, but there was still enough light to explore. I retraced my steps, scanning the edges of the meadow and the underbrush beyond it. After a few minutes of poking around, I spotted them—tiny purplish berries growing in loose bunches on leafy shrubs.

"Huckleberries!" I said, practically grinning. I picked a few and popped them into my mouth. Sweet, a little tart, and actually kind of perfect.

I gathered as many as I could, cupping them in my shirt like a bowl. As I walked back toward my makeshift camp, the sky above started to shift to orange and pink.

Sitting cross-legged again in the grass, I slowly ate the berries, savoring each one. It wasn't much, but it was enough for now.

The woods were quiet, except for the sound of a few crickets starting up. I lay back in some grass and looked up through the trees, thinking about how weirdly peaceful it all felt.

"Not bad," I whispered.

Then, like a pinprick in my thoughts, a new question popped up.

Wait... what if I'm lost?

CHAPTER II

THE CLIMB

I woke up to the light swoosh of the ocean, brushing against the side of the raft. Sitting up, I rubbed my eyes and took in the calm sea around me. The gentle rhythm was almost soothing.

This doesn't even feel like a dream anymore. It's like I'm living two lives, slipping between them every time I close my eyes.

"Guess I must've passed out," I muttered, stretching my arms until my shoulders cracked. "At least we didn't drift."

I peered out at the horizon. There it was—the island, clear and unmistakable, just as I remembered. Relief flooded through me as I grabbed the paddles and prepared to move.

"Well, better get to it," I said, sliding into position.

The sea was merciful today. The water shimmered under the rising sun, a golden hue reflecting off its surface. I paddled my heart out.

The island was a patch of lush green in the middle of the vast blue, alive with a vibrancy that seemed unreal. As I got closer, the trees came into view—tall, sturdy, and swaying gently in the breeze. It wasn't common to find palm trees this far north, but here they thrived, their bright green fronds catching the sunlight. The turquoise water lapping at its shores was so clear that I could see the ripples of the sand underneath.

When the boat scraped onto the soft, white sand, I jumped out and pulled it ashore, leaving a trail behind me. Grabbing the rope I'd saved, I tied the raft securely to a tree near the beach.

"Can't have my only ride floating away," I said, patting the rope knot with satisfaction.

I explored the island with cautious awe, my bare feet sinking into the sand as I walked. The vibrant greens of the forest contrasted perfectly with the soft blues and golds of the sea.

I wandered to a small tidal pool protected by the

palms. The water sparkled, and the smooth, colorful stones at the bottom gleamed like jewels.

"Wow," I breathed, taking it all in.

The more I looked around, the more I fell in love with the place. It wasn't just beautiful—it felt alive, almost like it was waiting for someone to claim it.

"I think I'll call it... the Jackdaw's Nest," I puffed my chest. "Yeah, that fits."

Curiosity tugged at me, and I continued exploring. Surrounding trees grew thicker and thicker. I made my way to the far side of the island, where the terrain became rockier, and the lush forest thinned out, revealing more of the surrounding sea. I found a large flat stone and sat down, letting the peace of the moment wash over me.

When I opened my eyes, something in the distance caught my attention.

A white manor perched high on a cliff, its walls bright against the dark greens and blues surrounding it. Below, at the base of the cliff, was a deep saltwater cave, its dark mouth contrasting against the shimmering waves.

I thought back to the old captain's map. He'd said we were far from any civilization. Was he wrong? Had he lied?

"Doesn't matter now." I shrugged off the

thought. The sight of the manor didn't worry me—it intrigued me. But there was no point in trying to reach the mainland tonight. It was growing dark, and I wanted to go back to the boat. Besides, I'll go there tomorrow.

I headed back to the tidal pool and the boat. Protected by the trees and close to fresh water. I gathered a few branches, leaned them against a sturdy tree, and padded the structure with leaves and forest debris.

I stared up at the sky, watching the stars appear one by one. "One day, when I have a family, I'll bring them here," I whispered. "They'd love it."

My eyelids grew heavier and I drifted off into a deep, dreamless sleep.

CHAPTER 12
THE MANOR'S GATES

When my eyes finally adjusted to the light, I rummaged through my backpack for something to eat. Pulling out a granola bar, I tore open the wrapper and took a big bite, savoring the simple pleasure of eating something fresh and unspoiled.

The warmth of the sun on my face and the satisfaction of a decent meal were almost enough to make me forget.

Almost.

As I sat there, a growing unease settled over me; the unfamiliar surroundings whispered of a place unknown, and I realized with a jolt that I was utterly lost.

Panic prickled at the edges of my mind. I stood,

turning in every direction, trying to spot something —anything—that looked familiar.

Nothing.

I turned again, only to be blinded by the sun, and that's when it hit me. A memory from school.

The sun rises in the east. "And the manor is to the north." If the sun was to my right, then north had to be... that way. I turned and looked up the hill, my pulse settling as the plan solidified in my mind.

After picking up my bag, I began walking, keeping the sun to my left as I wound my way through the forest. The further I walked, the more alive the forest seemed. Brightly colored birds flitted between the branches, their songs filling the air with a melody as cheerful as the sunlight. Squirrels darted through the underbrush, some small and sleek, others bushy and bold, their patterns as varied as the leaves above.

The trees themselves were a marvel. Tall and swaying gently in the breeze, their branches cast shifting rays of golden sunlight onto the forest floor. The light seemed to guide my steps, each beam a marker pointing me toward my destination.

After walking for what felt like hours, I stumbled upon a massive stone wall. It must have been six or seven feet high, built from weathered stone bricks that had aged beautifully over the years. Despite its age, the wall was solid, a testament to the craftsmanship of whoever had built it.

Every few feet, the design shifted slightly, alternating between stone bricks and layers of smooth stone slabs. The effect was mesmerizing, and I couldn't help but trail my fingers along the surface as I walked beside it.

I followed the wall for at least a mile before I finally came across the gate.

It rose majestically, towering at least twelve feet high. On either side, the wall arched upward, meeting the gate with an elegant curve.

The gate itself was a brilliant gold, its surface intricately designed. It depicted a grand manor perched on a point, overlooking an endless sea. Below, a pirate ship sailed the waves, its name etched clearly on the nameplate, The Jackdaw.

The craftsmanship of the gate was impressive; each meticulously carved detail spoke of a master craftsman's hand.

"So this is it," I murmured, placing a hand on the cool metal.

The Jackdaw's Nest.

I took a deep breath, my fingers tightening on the gate. Whatever lay beyond, I was ready to face it.

CHAPTER 13
MEET THE SHIFFS

I examined the intricately woven gate. Frustration bubbled up inside me. "How am I supposed to open it?" I paced back and forth.

Looking closer, I noticed something I hadn't seen before—a smaller door tucked near the base of the gate, just above the shoreline. It was easy to miss, blending seamlessly with the elaborate design.

Hesitantly, I turned the small, round, cool metal handle. A series of sharp clicks rang out, and I stepped back, startled.

To my amazement, the entire gate swung inward, moving with a deliberate grace. The gold bars shimmered in the sunlight, casting yellowish-gold highlights onto the driveway beyond.

A long, winding driveway stretched into the distance, perfectly paved and flanked by two rows of trees. The outer row was made up of vibrant maples, their fiery red and orange leaves swaying like dancers caught in a waltz. Behind them stood cherry blossom trees in full bloom, their pale pink petals drifting down in a delicate rain, catching the sunlight like tiny sparks.

It was enchanting, the colors vivid and alive. It was magic.

As I walked farther along the driveway, I couldn't help but marvel at the immaculate land-scaping. Every plant and tree looked as though it had been handpicked and cared for meticulously. Stone arch bridges spanned a sparkling stream, their paths wandering off into hidden corners of the estate. A pond reflected the sky like liquid mirrors, and perfectly trimmed grass stretched out, as if the earth itself had been polished for my arrival.

The closer I got to the house, the more unbeliev-able it became—as if I'd suddenly found myself at Disneyland.

Dazzling waterfalls flanked the driveway, cascading gracefully into small ponds on either side. Their streams wove down the hills, feeding into the landscape.

Then, there it was—a house. No, a manor.

The mansion was grand and unmistakably French in style. Its crisp white façade stood out against the natural colors of the landscape, accented with navy blue and gold trims that gleamed in the sunlight. Large windows lined the front of the house, each reflecting the brilliant surroundings.

The front yard was divided into three segments. The driveway curved around the middle, where a magnificent fountain stood—a sculpture of a bird's nest cradling a pirate ship. Water cascaded from the ship's sails, sparkling as it fell.

I made my way to the grand wooden doors at the center of the mansion, each carved with intricate depictions of the Jackdaw. My heart pounded as I raised my hand and knocked three times.

Bang, bang, bang.

For a moment, there was only silence. Then, the door opened. Standing in the entryway was a man who looked as though he'd stepped straight out of a storybook. Absolutely unreal.

He was tall and regal, with neatly combed gray hair and piercing blue eyes. He was impeccably dressed, wearing a crisp white shirt under a tight black vest, a small bow tie at his throat, black trousers, and polished shoes that gleamed like onyx.

Without hesitation, he stepped forward, bowing deeply. "Welcome home, Master James."

CHAPTER 14
MASTER JAMES SHIPMAN

A lump formed in my throat. I swallowed hard. My nerves tangled as I stood frozen in place.

"Um, pardon, but how do you know my name?" I asked, taking a cautious step back.

The man before me didn't answer immediately. Instead, he grabbed my hand, inspecting me closely, like a concerned doctor. "Oh, it's been far too long! How are you? Have those cursed foster parents been treating you well? I swear, if they've mistreated you, Master James—"

"Excuse me?" I pulled my hand back, slightly alarmed. "Who are you? How do you know about my foster parents?"

The man stepped back, straightened his posture,

and bowed deeply again. "Ah, forgive my manners. I admit, I've grown a bit rusty over the years. My name is Sebastian Schiff, your family's head butler."

"My family's... head butler?" I repeated, my words dragging as I tried to reconcile his words with my actual life.

"Yes, Master James," he said. "As head butler, I oversee all other household staff in your family's employ. Now, why don't you come inside? You must be tired."

His words sat uneasily in my mind, like a puzzle piece that didn't quite fit. Your family's employ? The phrasing struck me as odd, too formal—too detached. My pulse quickened, and for the first time, I wondered if stepping inside was a mistake.

Still, I forced myself to move, shuffling past him with stiff, mechanical steps. The air inside smelled of polished wood and something faintly floral. It was unfamiliar yet strangely inviting. My nerves prickled, a sharp current running beneath my skin —the same restless energy that came with meeting someone important, someone who could change everything. Still reeling from his words, I shuffled past him awkwardly, unsure of what to say or do. A jolt of pure adrenaline shot through me; my nerves felt like tightly wound springs.

All my tension melted away the moment I saw her.

She appeared like a vision, her presence lighting up the room with a brilliance that could rival the sun. My awkwardness faded like a wave washing over the shore.

"This is my daughter, Alysa Schiff," Sebastian said, gesturing toward her with a small smile. "She will show you around the manor, unless you'd like to explore on your own."

"Oh, um, that's fine," I stammered, unable to take my eyes off her.

Alysa had long, wavy brown hair that cascaded over her shoulders, hazel eyes that sparkled with kindness, and a smile so radiant it could brighten the darkest corners of the earth. There was something magnetic about her, an effortless beauty that left me feeling tongue-tied.

"Hello, Master James. It's a pleasure to meet you," she said in a voice so sweet it felt like it could charm even the sourest of souls.

"Oh, um, likewise," I mumbled, looking down at my feet. "And, uh, you can drop the 'Master' part."

Her smile widened, filling the room with warmth. "Oh, really? Thanks," Alysa said. "I hope we can become friends."

"Y-yeah, me too," I said, finally meeting her gaze.

Before I could think of what to say next, a woman rounded the corner from what appeared to be the kitchen. She was shorter than Sebastian, with long, curly brown hair and kind brown eyes.

"Lunch is almost ready," she announced warmly. "Alysa, why don't you help the young master get settled?"

"Yes, Mother," Alysa said, her voice carrying that same charming tone. She turned back to me, her smile unwavering. "Follow me, James."

I hesitated, glancing back at Sebastian. "Wait, there's still one thing I don't understand."

Sebastian stopped mid-step and turned to face me, his brow slightly raised in surprise. "Yes, Master James? What is it?"

"How do you know who I am?" I asked, my voice sharper now.

Sebastian's expression softened, and a small smile played at the corners of his lips. "Why, of course, we sent someone to watch over you, Master James."

"What?" I stared at him, my disbelief growing. "Who?"

"Think about it," Sebastian said calmly. "Who

was always there, checking on you, looking out for you? Always making sure you were safe?"

My mind raced, pieces of the puzzle falling into place. There was only one person who fit that description.

"Wait... Tom?"

CHAPTER 15
AT CLIFF'S EDGE

I stood, frozen. In the distance, I could make out the faint sound of silverware against plates.

"Tom?" I asked, my voice filled with disbelief.

"Yes," Sebastian said.

"But, but... I've known him for so long." My brain was racing.

"I can explain." Sebastian set down a plate of food in front of me. "Eat."

I looked down at my plate, momentarily stunned. I'd never seen such a feast—not in my life, anyway. A vibrant pile of freshly cut fruit glistened under the light. The small salad was a bright, leafy green. It looked crisp and delicate, with just a hint of what smelled like a tangy dressing on its surface.

And then there was the sandwich—thick slices of roast beef stacked between two pieces of golden bread, held together by a generous swipe of something that looked creamy. The scent of it all was almost overwhelming, savory and fresh in a way that made my stomach tighten in anticipation. I was salivating at the idea of biting into this sandwich. I nearly forgot what we were talking about when Sebastian broke my trance.

"You would have been eleven or twelve when we learned you were still alive after the car crash," Sebastian said, worry spreading across his face. "You were aware of the car crash, right?"

"Yes," I nodded, muttering through a full mouth.

"We weren't sure it was really you at the orphanage. When Mrs. Schiff and I submitted our adoption paperwork, someone informed us you were already spoken for."

"The Goodmans," I said.

Sebastian inclined his head. "We had no proof that you belonged here. Your great-grandfather and grandfather pressured your parents to keep important things... hidden. To bring you home, Mrs. Schiff and I opted to adopt you. But we were too late."

"What does that have to do with Tom?" I asked.

"Tom and his family work here at the manor as

well," he said. "He was about the right age, so when we found out where you were going to be enrolled in school, we sent Tom in to keep an eye on you. Until we could either find the paperwork that would bring you home or find another way."

"So, he lied? He's been pretending to be my friend this whole time?" I dropped my fork; melon rolled off the end of it and onto the table.

"No, he loves you. As far as I know, he's never lied to you," Sebastian said before grabbing my fork from the table and handing it back to me, his other hand gently patting me on the shoulder. "Tom was happy to find a friend like you."

I sighed. "I wish I could talk to him."

"You can," Sebastian said.

"I can?"

"Yes, he's here right now," Sebastian said with a sparkle in his eye. "I think he's in the study. Why don't you finish up, and Alysa will show you the way? You two can go say hi quickly before exploring a little."

I finished my sandwich and followed Alysa out of the kitchen. The plush crimson carpets offset the gleam of the granite hallways.

The doors to the study were dark oak, similar to the front doors with intricate carvings of the sea and a small island that looked like the Jackdaw's Nest. We pushed open the doors, and Tom turned to me casually as if it were perfectly normal for the two of us to be here together. "Oh, hey, Master James."

"Tom?" I said, approaching him. "What the hell?"

"I live here. Well, I also kind of work here. I'm a descendant of your family's butler service," Tom said.

"This is all so confusing and overwhelming," I said, gripping my head. It was almost too much to process.

"I understand. I'm the same old Tom. Just trust me, it's all going to be okay," he said more seriously than I had ever seen him.

"Why do you care? I was just a job," I said, turning my back on him.

"No! I was excited to go to school. I was excited to meet you. The first day I came home, I told my mom that I had found a best friend. The first day! I knew that you and I were going to be good friends," Tom said. "I only ever wanted to make sure you were okay."

His words pinballed through my mind. I fell backward. Thankfully, there was a chair to catch me.

"Please, trust my parents and me when I say that we only ever meant the best for you," Tom said.

"Why couldn't you just tell me?" I asked.

"There's more at play than you realize. We couldn't tell you who you were. It could have jeopardized everything," Tom said.

"Okay, you've been my best friend for years. I trust you." I saw the relief in his face. "But no more secrets, okay?"

"Absolutely," he grinned.

I felt a gentle tug on my arm, pulling me toward the door.

"Why don't we go on our tour? I can explain some more and show you around. We can catch up with Tom later," Alysa said.

"Oh, okay," I said, as a cheerful tug pulled me out of the room.

When I looked up, we were outside; the sun was shining brightly above us. Alysa stood in front of me, her smile radiant and warm. From my angle, the sun framed her head like a glowing halo, her wavy brown hair flowing gently in the breeze.

"Ready, James?" she asked, her voice light and filled with excitement.

Feeling a little bit foolish, I couldn't help but smile back. "Yep. What's first?"

"Let's explore the outside! I bet you'll love the backyard," she said, grabbing my hand and pulling me along.

A split ran down the middle of the roof, its long side facing the driveway. The structure had two floors, with large windows evenly spaced across the front. The doors, painted navy blue and trimmed in gold, adorned each side of the house, but the back was the real showstopper.

A grand arch framed the back French doors, flanked by two massive windows with a backyard view. And what a backyard it was.

A vast field stretched out, surrounded by colorful garden beds brimming with vibrant blooms. Pink, yellow, and purple flowers danced in the breeze, their colors merging in a vibrant display.

"Isn't it beautiful, James?" Alysa said, turning slightly to face me. She stood with the breeze catching her hair and dress, both moving with an elegance that made her look like she belonged in a painting.

"Yeah, truly beautiful," I replied, though to be honest, I wasn't really looking at the field.

Alysa smiled, her hazel eyes glinting with amusement. "You know, I have a lot of reasons for loving this yard, but my favorite is that it reminds me of your eyes."

"Oh, um, thanks..." I stammered, feeling my cheeks heat. I'd never thought about my eyes—or anything about my appearance, really. I'd always assumed I was just another face in the crowd, but here she was, complimenting me.

A melodic giggle escaped her lips. "Come on, J. Follow me."

She led me to the edge of the property, where the ground sloped down to a cliff overlooking the ocean.

In the distance, an island rested on the horizon, its shape familiar.

"I think I've seen that island before..." I said, squinting to get a better look.

"It's one of your family's properties," Alysa said, sitting down gracefully in the grass. "Actually, I think it might have been the first one." A warm expression accompanied her words, one I couldn't quite explain, but I felt it deeply.

"Oh, yeah, I guess so," I said, sitting down beside her. "Hey, what's your favorite color? If you don't mind me asking."

She smiled, playing with the grass. "Hmm, I think it's green—kind of like your eyes."

"Yeah, I guess I like green too," I replied, my voice softer now. "But your eyes are pretty, too."

She looked up at me, her cheeks faintly pink. "Thanks. Hey, have you ever gone sailing?"

My face lit up. "Yeah! I loved it. Wait—have you sailed before?"

Her hazel eyes sparkled with excitement. "Oh, yes! It was amazing. The wind in your face, the sea glittering under the sun... It's like a giant sapphire crystal."

Hours passed like minutes with Alysa. She showed me all of her favorite places around the manor.

Ding. Ding. Ding.

A bell echoed across the property, interrupting the moment. Alysa stood, brushing off her dress.

"What's going on?" I asked, slightly alarmed.

"It's dinnertime," she said with a soft laugh. "A shame, though. I wish we had more time to talk about the sea together. Maybe tomorrow?"

Dinner was so exquisite that tears welled in my eyes after the first bite. It wasn't just delicious—it felt like a celebration of a life I could have one day.

Afterward, Alysa showed me to a grand room overlooking the backyard. She handed me a set of clothes, including a crisp white shirt, a black dress vest, a red tie, and black dress pants for tomorrow.

As I prepared for bed, I caught my reflection in the large mirror by the wardrobe.

My short brown hair was tousled into small, messy tufts, not curly, but not entirely straight either. My green eyes looked bigger and brighter than I'd realized, and my skin, despite its years of neglect, was clear except for a few freckles dotting my cheeks.

Maybe I'll try to clean up tomorrow. I glanced down at the neatly folded clothes Alysa had given me. "Not because she said anything, of course. That'd be silly."

Shaking my head, I crawled into the enormous bed. The soft blankets and plush pillows surrounded me, and I let myself drift into a peaceful sleep, the day's events replaying in my mind like a dream.

CHAPTER 16
THE BARON'S REVENGE

I opened my eyes to a picturesque island, the sun rising over the horizon and casting golden hues across the calm ocean. I was still wearing the blue vest embroidered with a gold jackdaw, its wings spread in mid-flight—a symbol that felt more important every time I saw it.

"Right, time to explore that manor." I shook off the ache of the morning and headed toward the raft I'd tied up earlier. Gathering my supplies, I piled the essentials onto the raft and stashed the rest at my temporary camp.

"I'll be back, Nest." I smiled, pushing the raft off the shore and paddling toward the mainland. The water was glass-like. Looking over the side of the boat, the sight of a man startled me. I was still not quite used to having two bodies—the one where I'm him and the one where I'm me.

The journey was smooth at first, the gentle rhythm of the paddle soothing against the backdrop of the glittering water. But as I got closer to the mainland, stronger currents pulled along the shore, forcing me to work harder. My ribs ached in agony. Between the boat sinking and getting beaten by Derrick, I couldn't tell why I hurt anymore. I just did. That meant I struggled to keep pace with the lapping waves.

Once I reached the rocky coast, my heart sank. The cliff loomed above me like an insurmountable wall, and I wasn't sure how I'd get up. But then I spotted an old, worn-down stone staircase winding its way up the side of the cliff.

"Well, that's convenient," I muttered, tying the raft to a nearby tree and stashing my remaining supplies behind a bush. The staircase looked steep, and I knew hauling everything up in one go wasn't an option.

The stone staircase was uneven. A wrong step and I'd tumble back down. I began the arduous ascent. I made it all of ten steps before my foot slipped, almost sending me back down.

"Well, that would've sucked." I let out a breath.

"Get it together, Shipman." About halfway up the cliffside, I couldn't take it anymore and stopped to rest. Steep no longer felt like the right way to describe this climb. Sheer? Precipitous? Perpendicular!

I sat on the steps, catching my breath. The view was devastating—endless turquoise-blue meeting the horizon in a seamless blend.

Worth every single blister this damned cliff has caused. I stretched my arms while rolling my neck to loosen a knot that had formed, then checked my feet, relieved to find no blisters. "I suppose that's a relief."

Slipping my shoes back on, I continued the climb. The path remained long and tedious, but the greenery slowly encapsulating me the closer to the top I climbed softened the effort. Overgrown trees formed a natural canopy, and wildflowers in full bloom now decorated the edges of the staircase.

Finally, after what felt like hours, I reached the top. The sight of the manor stole the air from my lungs. Despite its age, the grand house stood in remarkably good condition—nothing some hard work and a bit of love couldn't fix. I peeked through a window and was met with white walls and navy-blue trim. It hinted at what lay beyond if I could get in through the door.

"Heave ho, heave ho," I grunted, pushing against the massive wooden door at the front.

The door gave way with a sudden groan that sent me sprawling to the floor.

"Ah!" I yelped, brushing myself off as I stood. Dust clung to my clothes, but I didn't care. The interior of the manor was just as grand as the exterior.

As I wandered through the house, I marveled at its preserved beauty. High ceilings, ornate moldings, and antique furniture gave it an almost regal atmosphere.

In what appeared to be a large office, or library, a large bookshelf caught my eye. It was filled with leather-bound titles of all sizes and colors, their spines worn from use. One in particular stood out— Pirateering for Beginners.

Curious, I reached for the book, but instead of pulling out, it tilted forward, and the entire book-shelf slid to the side with a loud whoosh.

There was a HIDDEN STAIRCASE! Excitement bubbled in my chest.

The narrow stone steps spiraled downward, disappearing into the darkness below.

One step and the old wood gave way beneath my

foot. Before I could react, I was tumbling down the stairs. I reached the bottom with a heavy thud, dazed and disoriented.

I rubbed my eyes in disbelief. I must have hit my head or something. There was no way... I sat up slowly, orienting myself.

Before me was a massive underground cavern, and at its center was an enormous pirate ship. The name etched across its bow gleamed in the dim light: The Baron's Revenge.

"Who lived here?" My words were no more than a whisper. I moved to get a closer look, but before I could get far, the world went black and I fell into the abyss.

Into nothing.

CHAPTER 17
HAPPY LOOKS BEST IN REAL LIFE

An unexpected knock at the door grabbed my attention. "Master James, may I come in?" a voice called from outside my door.

I jolted awake, my heart racing as I scrambled out of bed. "I'm sorry! I'll get right to the chores," I blurted, pulling on my old, tattered clothes and rushing to the door.

When I swung it open, Alysa stood there, her head tilted in confusion. "What chores?"

"Oh, um... nothing," I said, my cheeks heating with embarrassment as I avoided her gaze.

Alysa's face softened, her eyes sparkling with amusement. "Will you eat breakfast with us today?"

Her tone was so warm it eased my nerves almost instantly. "Oh, yeah, I'd love to, but what about the chores?" I asked, glancing around nervously.

"You don't need to do chores here," she said with a big, comforting smile. "If you're eating with us, please follow me." She turned gracefully and started down the hallway.

"Oh, um, if you don't mind... where's the bathroom?" I asked, stopping awkwardly.

"Down the hall, third door on the right. Do you know your way to the main dining hall?" she asked, standing up straighter as she spoke.

"Yes, I think so. Thank you," I said, grateful.

"Of course." With that, she turned and continued on her way, her steps light and full of purpose.

The hallway leading to the bathroom looked like something straight out of a royal castle. A plush red carpet ran down the middle of the polished stone floor, flanked by walls of perfectly fitted gray stone bricks. Beautiful tapestries hung at evenly spaced intervals, each one depicting a scene that hinted at stories long forgotten.

I opened the large white bathroom door and entered a room that could only be described as opulent. The floor was polished gray stone, and the walls matched, stretching outward endlessly. It had to be at least fifty feet in each direction, with gold fixtures gleaming in the morning light.

After freshening up, I made my way downstairs, rounding a corner just as laughter echoed through the hall. I paused, staying out of sight so I could peek at the voices.

Sebastian was teasing Alysa about something, his voice low and lighthearted. Alysa, smiling but clearly flustered, tried unsuccessfully to make him stop talking. Meanwhile, Emily, Alysa's mother, sat watching them with a warm laugh that filled the room. It was such a simple moment—a family enjoying each other's company—it made my chest tighten.

Once the commotion settled, I stepped around the corner. "What's for breakfast?" I asked, doing my best to sound casual as I walked toward the table.

Emily rose and gave a small bow. "Eggs Benedict with hollandaise sauce, ham, and arugula on a classic English muffin," she said.

"Oh, you don't need to do that," I said quickly, gesturing for her to sit back down. "Really, I know you apparently served my family, but please, treat me normally."

"Of course," she said with a kind smile, settling

back into her chair. I moved to sit next to Alysa before overloading my plate. It all smelled so delicious. I'd never seen eggs with a sauce before, but it smelled good enough to bathe in.

"So, how'd you sleep?" Emily asked as she poured me a glass of orange juice.

"I've been having weird dreams for a couple of weeks. Realistic and intense, actually. But other than that, I slept better than I have, possibly ever before." I smiled before taking my first bite of breakfast. The eggs and hollandaise sauce melted in my mouth like butter, and the muffin, ham, and arugula paired perfectly, each bite balanced. It was like learning the world had color for the first time. I'd forgotten that food could taste good. More than just sustenance, it was joyful.

"This is delicious," I said between mouthfuls, my enthusiasm earning a soft laugh from Alysa.

"Hey, James," she said, leaning in closer.

"Yeah?"

"I have something you might want to see," she said, her tone teasing as she leaned back and gave me a mysterious smile.

CHAPTER 18
PIRATEERING FOR BEGINNERS

"So what's the big surprise?" I asked, following Alysa to an enormous library.

"You'll see," she sang.

"Man, I could really just get lost in here for ages," I said, brushing my fingertips across the leather spines.

"Yeah, I get that. Sometimes I crawl into the green leather couch there," Alysa pointed, "and read for hours."

"What's your favorite?"

She thought for a moment and then walked over to a book titled Pirateering for Beginners. Before she reached for it, I remembered—that was the book from my dream. I had pulled it, and before I could finish the thought, the unmistakable sound of a secret door sliding open rang out.

Alysa pulled at the copy of Pirateering for Beginners, revealing a dark staircase behind it. These stairs—they were also in my dream.

The passage led downward, stairs spiraling into the earth. The walls were rough, carved out like a mineshaft, with jagged edges that caught the dim light. The stairs themselves groaned underfoot, each step sounding more precarious than the last. Alysa lit the way with an old oil lamp she had taken from a metal spike embedded in the wall at the entrance to the cavern. The warm glow illuminated her face, casting flickering shadows that danced across the walls.

When we reached the bottom of the staircase, my jaw literally dropped.

Before us stretched a vast underground cave, its mouth opening directly into the ocean. The water shimmered with a deep lapis blue, a stark contrast to the warm yellow light spilling from rows of oil lamps fixed along the rocky walls. And there, dominating the cavern like a sleeping giant, was a massive pirate ship.

"The Baron's Revenge," I read. The name was painted in bold white letters along its hull.

"Amazing, isn't it?" Alysa said, her voice almost reverent.

I turned to look at her, seeing the awe in her expression mirrored in my own. "Yeah," I whispered. "It's incredible."

I couldn't help myself—I started walking toward the ship, drawn to its overwhelming presence like a moth to a flame. Alysa snapped out of her daze and quickly followed, her lamp swaying in her hands.

The ship rested alongside a long wooden dock, also lit by oil lamps. A boarding ramp stretched up to the main deck, its wooden planks sturdy and weathered. As I climbed, I noted the ship's design in greater detail. Someone had painted its hull black with intricate gold edges. Its towering sails were a deep, regal purple.

"This is a 124-gun man o' war," Alysa said behind me.

"Have you ever sailed on it?" I asked.

"No," she admitted with a hint of sadness in her voice. "We've never had enough people to crew it. You'd need at least seven hundred and fifty, maybe nine hundred, to operate a ship like this properly."

"Maybe during wartime," I said, my mind racing with possibilities. "But for just a pleasure cruise, you could probably operate it with fifty or a hundred people. How many staff members do we have on the estate?"

"About twenty," she replied, stumbling slightly as she caught up to me on the ramp.

"Could we hire more?" I asked as we reached the top.

"I suppose we could, but housing, paying, and feeding them would be a challenge," she said thoughtfully.

I nodded, my excitement tempered by the practicalities. "I'll talk to Sebastian later."

The deck was crafted from polished dark wood, its rich surface managing to sparkle, even in this cave. The masts rose high above us, their edges lined with delicate gold trim. Such an addition to the ship's design imparted an air of sophisticated royal elegance. Despite its beauty, there was an unmistakable edge to the ship, a sense of danger lurking beneath its elegance.

As I moved toward the steering wheel of the ship, my fingers brushed against the cool, smooth wood, and I gazed out at the seemingly endless expanse of the ship's deck. I knew just outside this cave, the vastness of the ocean stretched out before me, its deep blue waters merging seamlessly with the sky on the distant horizon.

For a moment, I was transported back to my dreams, imagining the days when this ship was filled with the hustle and bustle of sailors going about their duties. A gust of wind blew from behind me, carrying with it the echoes of voices long past. I strained to hear the words.

"Pick up your bootstraps and raise the sails, you bunch of scurvy dogs and scallywags!" a dark, commanding voice seemed to echo in my mind. The image of a grizzled captain barking orders to his crew flashed before my eyes, and I couldn't help but smile at the vividness.

Rain lashed against the deck, drumming in an erratic rhythm. I closed my eyes and let myself be enveloped by the sounds of the sea.

"Sir, yes, sir, Captain Jack!" The response came like a thunderclap, a hundred voices shouting in unison.

"I can't hear you, landlubbers!"

"Sir, yes, sir, Captain Jack," the voices roared back, doubling in intensity. But the voices blurred, the sounds fading like a distant storm.

When I opened my eyes again, I was back on the ship, with Alysa by my side. I blinked, the echoes of voices still ringing in my ears, lingering like the salty mist in the air. My fingers flexed against the wheel, steadying myself as reality settled back in. Alysa leaned against the railing, watching me with a knowing smirk.

"You felt it, didn't you?" she asked.

I exhaled sharply, shaking my head. "I don't know what I felt."

She chuckled, her gaze sweeping over the deck and out toward the endless horizon. "It's the call of the sea. Freedom, adventure—everything you've ever wanted, waiting just beyond the next wave."

I studied her face. There was something almost wistful in her expression, like she was seeing beyond the ship, beyond the bay—somewhere far greater than this moment.

"Do you really think being a pirate would be great?" I asked.

She turned to me, eyes shining. "Of course! Imagine it. No rules, no one telling you what to do, just the open sea stretching forever in front of you. Every day, a new opportunity. Treasure to be found, ships to board, legends to write in the tides." She leaned closer, lowering her voice like she was letting me in on some great secret. "You ever think about it? What it'd be like out there, living that kind of life?"

I let my fingers trail along the wheel, considering. "Definitely."

She laughed. "Oh, come on. Piracy runs through your veins. It's in your blood. I'd be shocked if you hadn't."

I hesitated, my grip tightening on the wheel. "I don't know if 'piracy' is the right word," I muttered.

Alysa raised an eyebrow. "Isn't it, though? Your great-grandfather was the greatest pirate in the western world. No one could ever pin a single crime on him!"

I glanced at her. "What do you know about him?"

"Well," she said with a grin, "he built a legacy that no one could touch. Took this old manor, restored it to its former glory, and raised his family like noblemen—while secretly ruling the seas."

I exhaled slowly, the weight of history settling over me. I had heard the stories in school about the famed Captain Jack Shipman. Even though we shared a surname, I never considered it could be family lore. However, hearing it from Alysa made it feel different—more real.

We wandered back towards the gangway. Right at the door at the edge of the ship, I noticed something carved into the wood. I leaned in and read it out loud. "The sea belongs to those who dare to take it."

Alysa nodded. "And he took it without hesitation." She leaned back, gazing out at the water. "The question is...what about you?"

I swallowed, the wind whipping around us. Somewhere in the distance, the waves crashed against the shore, a rhythmic pulse, steady and strong. I wasn't sure I had an answer yet.

CHAPTER 19
SHRIMP RISOTTO

"So, what's for dinner?" I asked, leaning casually against the doorframe. Alysa and I were back upstairs in the manor. My stomach growled, and she insisted on going back for a meal.

"I was thinking of making shrimp risotto with mushrooms, chopped green onion, and a shredded parmesan garnish. How does that sound?" Alysa asked, turning back to glance at me as she entered the kitchen, her face glowing with enthusiasm.

"Sounds great. Mind if I help? I actually have some experience cooking," I offered, though I wasn't about to tell her that the Goodmans had forced me to make dinner every night, only to leave me with scraps from meals long past their prime.

"Oh, really? What kind of experience?" Alysa asked, her curiosity piqued.

"Oh, you know, just helping out in the kitchen now and then," I replied, dodging the truth with a casual shrug.

"Well, why don't you start by getting the ingredients? I'll sharpen the knife," she said, pulling a blade from the wooden block and testing its edge.

"Got it." I headed to the fridge and began gathering the cooking wine, broth, mushrooms, and a few other essentials, leaving some items for the later steps. "When did you learn to cook?"

"I took an interest when I was six," she said, taking the mushrooms and setting them on the cutting board.

"That's young. Was it your choice?" I asked, handing her a bulb of garlic.

"Yes, of course. Well, kind of." Alysa thought for a moment, gathering her thoughts. "My family has been serving this property for as long as it's been in your family. I've lived here my whole life."

I nodded along, but didn't interrupt her. She was expertly slicing the mushrooms before tossing them into a pan with a splash of cooking wine.

"School is my priority right now, and being a teenager. But it's in my blood the same way that the ocean moves through you. I thought it would be neat, though, to learn to cook a few enjoyable meals before your return."

"Why did you have to learn to cook for my return?" I asked, puzzled.

"Well, if I want to go into the family business, there's a lot to learn," she said with a small smile while sautéing the mushrooms.

"Do you like being here? Or do you wish you could do something different?" I asked, concern creeping into my voice.

"James," she said, pausing to look at me. "I'm an independent woman, and I get to decide what I want to do with my life. If I want to take on the noble responsibility of serving this household, I will. If I want to sail around the world and marry an Italian yacht captain, I will. I control my destiny." Alysa met my eyes. "But for the record, I've never not wanted to be here. Actually, I'm grateful I am, because if I wasn't, well...we wouldn't have met." She glanced away shyly, her cheeks blooming faintly pink.

"Oh...yeah, I guess that's true," I said, turning back to prep the remaining ingredients, a small smile tugging at my lips.

For the next hour, we worked side by side seamlessly. Once the dish was complete, I could enjoy the fruits of my labor and actually eat what I made—something that hadn't happened in recent memory, or distant memory for that matter. It was better than I could have imagined. The risotto was creamy, the shrimp perfectly cooked, and the flavors balanced in a way that made every bite feel like a celebration.

Later, after dinner, I talked to Sebastian about manning The Baron's Revenge. He said it might actually be possible with some adjustments.

The fire crackled softly in the grand fireplace. I sat on the edge of a leather couch, elbows resting on my knees, my mind still reeling. Sebastian stood near the mantel, his hands folded neatly in front of him, watching me with measured patience.

"This isn't a permanent solution, you know," he finally said, his voice even but firm.

I let out a slow breath, nodding. "I know."

"The Goodmans won't stop looking for you," Sebastian said flatly. "And with Pam's father being the chief of police, avoiding them would be...difficult, to say the least."

Difficult.

That was putting it mildly. I could already picture them scheming, pulling strings, making sure I had nowhere to run.

"I don't regret leaving," I said after a moment. "But I don't know what I'm supposed to do next."

Sebastian studied me for a long moment. Then, as if weighing his words carefully, he spoke. "The person who built all of this—the estate, the ship, everything—was your great-grandfather. We'll find a way to prove that and make sure you get to stay here, where you belong. You know, Captain Jack wasn't just a pirate."

I raised an eyebrow.

"He was a strategist. A survivor. He knew when to fight and when to vanish into the mist," Sebastian said. "A trait passed down in your family from generation to generation."

I let my eyes drift across the room, taking in the details—the old maps on the walls, the heavy wooden bookshelves, the glint of gold on the antique clock above the fireplace. I wondered how this place existed and lasted.

"What do I do?" I asked, knowing the answer.

Sebastian's lips curved ever so slightly. "That, Master James, is for you to discover."

The fire crackled again, and for the first time

since I'd left, I felt something settle in my chest. Not quite certainty, but a whisper of something close.

A direction.

A choice.

And a legacy waiting to be reclaimed.

CHAPTER 20
WHAT COULD
HAVE BEEN

The sound of knocking pulled me halfway out of a dream.

"James, wake up," a voice called from the other side of the door. "It's time to get up." The noise cut through the grogginess clouding my head.

As Alysa shook me awake, I gasped, snapping back to reality from whatever dream I'd been lost in.

"Oh, so you're finally awake," she said, arms crossed and scowling. "You promised you'd explore the property with me today. Were you planning to make me wait all day?"

I sat up slowly, blinking back the sunlight streaming through the open window. The curtains danced in the gentle breeze, and a soft, floral fragrance wafted in—sweet and comforting.

"What time is it?" I asked.

"It's well past time to rise and shine."

For a moment, her words made my heart thrum. If Derek or Pam had caught me in bed, I'd be walking funny for a week. Old habits die hard, as they say. But I'm not on that old cot. I'm in the manor. I took in a slow breath to calm my racing heart.

"Well, get dressed, space cadet," Alysa said, spinning on her heel and walking out of the room.

I swung my legs off the bed, stretching. After sitting there for a moment to shake off the last remnants of sleep, I finally got up and dressed.

I chose black pants with a matching belt, a crisp white button-up shirt, and a purple tie embroidered with a thin black pattern. I finished it off with a vest that matched the tie.

"I'm ready," I sang out, stepping into the hallway. "Now, what do you want to do?"

Alysa was waiting just outside my door. "About time." She raised an eyebrow and looked me up and down. "Now come on." Before I could react, she grabbed the cuff of my shirt and began pulling me along.

"Where are we going?" I asked, catching up and walking beside her. Even though I'd matched her pace, she didn't let go of my shirt.

I didn't mind.

"I want to show you this place in the woods, near the edge," Alysa said, picking up speed without glancing back.

"What do you mean by the edge?" I asked, trying to keep up with her pace.

"You remember the cliff we went to the other night? It's along there," she said, hopping over a fallen log while still holding onto me.

"Yeah, I remember. But what's so special about this spot?" I asked.

"You'll see." She grinned, but as she turned to look at me, she stumbled into a hole hidden by the brush.

Her grip on my shirt slipped as she started to fall. Instinctively, I reached out and grabbed her hand just in time to stop her from hitting the ground.

"You okay? You need to watch where you're walking," I said, pulling her back to her feet.

"Thanks," she said, sitting down on a nearby log to collect herself.

"Isn't that the cliff's edge over there?" I asked, pointing through the trees.

"Yeah, that's the spot," she said, standing and

brushing herself off. This time, she moved more carefully.

The cliff overlooked the ocean, its shimmering blue waters stretching endlessly into the horizon. Just offshore, the island was close enough to make out the small saltwater lake at its center, glinting in the sunlight like a jewel.

"Wow, it's beautiful," I said, staring at the view in awe.

"I know, right?" Alysa said, stepping closer to the edge.

"Thank you for bringing me here." I turned to face her.

"Of course. I thought you'd like it," she said, her smile warm and sincere.

My expression grew more serious. "Can I ask you something? About my family."

"Sure. What's up?" Alysa's smile faded into a look of concern.

"I've been wondering... what happened to my parents?" I asked.

Alysa hesitated, a shadow of sadness crossing her face. "James... they both died in a car accident when you..."

"No, no, sorry. I know about the accident. I

mean, did they live here too?" That could have been phrased better.

"Yes." Her voice was gentle, but the weight of her words pressed down on me like a lead blanket. Her face softened with sympathy as she waited for me to process what she'd just said. "But there's something you should know..."

"Okay," I said, bracing myself for any absolution.

"About the car crash..." she paused and looked away. "There are rumors that it wasn't an accident. Some evidence pointed to the possibility it was a setup."

My jaw dropped. I couldn't believe the words I was hearing.

"Apparently, the responding officer—who is now the chief—was the first on the scene," she continued. "Well, I don't know all the details, but apparently there were a lot of inconsistencies in their story."

"What do you mean?"

"The report shows that there were two dead and one missing. Then, in another report, it shows that there were three dead," she raised her eyebrows, waiting for my reaction.

"Right. I was the one missing. I was found by

some old lady later on that day," I explained. "Who was dead?"

"No, the report said that two were dead, a female and a child. Then, later it says all three occupants were deceased. Meaning a man and a woman, and a child," Alysa said. "So, it sounds like there was a mistake about you being at the scene or not."

"That doesn't make sense." I tried to wrap my head around what she was trying to tell me. "It could have been a typo."

"Yeah, it could have been. But I think there was more to the story. I don't remember all the details," she admitted.

We sat in a comfortable silence as I tried to make sense of this new information.

"Did you know them?" I asked, finally.

"I was very young. I don't remember them," she admitted.

"Of course," I said shyly. "I'm sorry. I didn't mean..."

"It's okay," she said, patting my shoulder. "I'm sure you could ask my parents. They'll tell you anything you want to know."

I nodded, but the unease in my chest didn't fade. It was strange—standing here, staring at the house that had once been theirs, knowing they had walked the same halls, lived in the same rooms. And yet, I had no real connection to it. To them.

Alysa must have noticed my hesitation because she tilted her head slightly, studying me. "Are you okay?"

I let out a slow breath. "I don't know. It just feels... off."

"How so?" she asked, her tone careful.

Hesitantly, I struggled to find the words. "I don't know. I guess I always imagined them in a normal house, not... this," I said, gesturing at the manor. "It's hard to picture them here. I don't even know if they were happy."

Alysa was quiet for a moment. "Maybe that's something worth finding out."

I glanced at her. "How?"

"Ask my parents!" she laughed.

A deep chuckle escaped my lips. "Yeah, yeah... I just want to know the truth."

Alysa nodded. There was something playful in her expression. "Then let's find out."

She grabbed me by the hand, and we headed back to the manor.

CHAPTER 21
RETURN

After hearing the slightly surprising news about my parents, I agreed to ask Sebastian about them after dinner. Alysa never left my side. She seemed to try her best to console me, but if I were being honest, I wasn't as shaken by it as she probably thought.

"James, are you sure you're okay? It's okay to be sad," Alysa said gently.

I turned to face her, meeting her eyes. "Yeah, I'm okay. Really. Thanks, though."

"Okay," she said, giving me a small, concerned smile, holding her hands up in surrender.

"Hey, Alysa..."

She had already started walking away but turned back to me. "Yeah?"

"To be honest, I don't want to sound cold or anything, but in the orphanage, I already kind of made peace with the fact that my parents were dead. I just wanted to know more about them. So, I'm okay, really." I smiled as warmly as I could.

"That may be true, but it's still okay to grieve," she said.

After dinner, Alysa and I helped clean up the dishes. She tried to get me to stop, but I insisted. Sebastian and Emily had disappeared to take care of other things around the manor.

"Are you ready to find my dad and talk about your parents?" Alysa asked as she rinsed the last piece of silverware.

"Yes, I think so." I felt a tightening in my chest.

We wandered around the manor, searching for Sebastian. We rounded the corner to a room I hadn't explored yet. There was so much to see, I think it could take a year to see every inch of this place.

The library was enormous—way bigger than any I'd ever seen, even at school. The ceiling stretched ridiculously high, with these massive wooden beams crisscrossing overhead like something out of an old adventure movie. Floor-to-ceiling bookshelves lined the walls, packed so tight with books that it almost felt like they were holding up the entire room. A rolling ladder stood off to the side—the kind you only ever see in movies, like some old professor was about to slide across the shelves in search of a long-lost secret.

I realized now that the room I thought was the library was probably just someone's personal office. Because while it contained a secret passage, this blew that collection out of the water.

The air smelled like old paper, leather, and just a little bit of dust, like no one had actually sat and read anything in a while. A massive fireplace dominated one wall, with a big, worn-out armchair in front of it. There sat Sebastian, reading by the firelight. Heavy curtains framed the window behind him, filtering the moonlight into a warm, white glow that made the whole place feel stuck in time.

I ran my fingers along the edge of one of the bookshelves. It was carved with these deep swirls and patterns, like someone had taken the time to make even the furniture feel important.

"Oh, Master James," Sebastian said, looking up from his book. "I didn't see you there."

He folded the book, set it on the arm of the chair, and stood up.

"Oh, I didn't mean to interrupt," I said.

"Nonsense. What can I do for you?" he said.

"Nothing. I was..." I looked around the room and found a book of maps on a nearby shelf. I reached out and grabbed it. "Was just looking for this. I wanted to study some maps."

"You sure?" he said, raising an eyebrow.

"Absolutely." I shuffled my way back out the door. "Goodnight then," I said, turning to go into my room.

"Goodnight, Master James," Sebastian said before heading back to his book.

I couldn't bring myself to ask about my parents. I don't know why. It just wasn't the right time.

The next morning, I woke up to sounds drifting up from downstairs.

Throwing the covers off, I got out of bed and pulled my clothes off the rack in the large wooden cabinet. I dressed as quickly as I could, curiosity bubbling up inside me.

I wonder what we're going to do today. I've barely explored a fraction of the grounds.

I rushed into the bathroom, brushing my teeth and taming my hair in record time. Shutting the door behind me, I bolted out of my room and pulled the door shut with a loud bang.

I made my way to the grand staircase, leaping onto the railing and sliding down. When I reached the bottom, I stumbled off the rail and landed ungracefully on the polished floor.

Raising my head, I expected to see the smiling faces of Alysa and her family. But what I saw instead stopped me cold.

Standing in the grand entrance were Pam and Derrick Goodman.

Their fake smiles were plastered onto their faces, oozing the same false sweetness I had grown to dread.

Alysa rounded the corner. When she caught sight of me, frozen in place, her expression turned to concern. She looked at me, confused, as I stood there trembling.

Ice-cold fear laced its way through my body. My legs felt like lead, unable to move. But somehow, they still shook under the weight of my dread. My mouth opened, but all that came out was a silent, repetitive whisper:

"Goodmans... Goodmans... Goodmans..."

"Come now, James. It's time to come home," Pam said, her voice as smooth and sweet as honey, but underneath it was a venom meant for me.

I couldn't move, but my body betrayed me, stepping forward toward them, one heavy step at a time.

Alysa called out to me, her voice distant and muffled, as if I were underwater.

As I crossed the threshold, the last thing she saw of me was a single tear rolling down my cheek—a solitary drop escaping from eyes that had gone dull, void of emotion, as all the light inside me went out.

CHAPTER 22
RESULT OF DISOBEDIENCE

Derrick's fist hit the wall with a crash, creating a hole in the drywall.

"You useless boy! I bet you think you're so clever," Derrick growled, pacing in front of me, his fists clenching and unclenching like he couldn't decide whether to punch the wall again—or me.

I sat there, bracing myself as he launched into another tirade about how much trouble I caused. The hits came hard and fast, kicks driving into my ribs as he leaned in close, yelling in my face. Why did I ever think paradise could last? My luck had allowed nothing good to stay. Life taught me that lesson early.

You know, I almost wished Derrick would finally

kill me. At least then, this nightmare would end. And with that last thought, the world went black.

When I came to, I was back in the basement. This nightmare won't end. My old cot was gone, replaced by the hard, cold ground. A sticky warmth dripped off my face and onto my clothes, sliding down my cheeks like Satan's honey spilling over my head. My stomach felt hollower than a bottomless cavern, but first, I had to deal with the blood pooling faster than someone running from trouble.

Tearing off a piece of my already ruined pants, I gently wrapped it around my battered forehead. The touch made me gasp, pain shooting through my skull like needles. Tears welled in my eyes, but I refused to let them fall.

"What are you doing?" came a low and chilling voice.

I froze, glancing around for one of the Goodmans. The room was empty.

"I know you can hear me, James," the disembodied voice said. It was so clear. Dare I say, almost mocking. "Get out of here."

"What?" I croaked, my voice hoarse.

"Let yourself out." This was a venomous hiss. "End your suffering."

Wind howled, and suddenly I was no longer

in the basement—I was back on the island, standing on the rocky shore. Rain lashed down in sharp, stinging darts, and the manor loomed in the distance like a shadowy beacon in the storm.

"You think they'll save you?" the voice sneered, riding the wind as it whipped around me. "How foolish can you be? You said it yourself—nothing good lasts. You're alone, Jack. Always have been."

"Who are you?" I shouted, my words ripped apart by the storm as waves crashed violently against the rocks.

"You thought it was destiny, that your pain was over. You thought they could help you," the voice taunted, fading and swirling with the storm. "How naïve. You're nothing but a shameful idiot."

"Stop!" I cried, desperate to silence the hate. "Who are you? Leave me alone!"

"Who am I?" the voice asked, sinister and amused.

A tear ripped through the storm—a jagged, glowing red rift in the gray-toned world. Through it, a figure began to crawl, shrouded in mist and shadow.

Bloodied hands gripped the edges of the tear, pulling the demon forward as the storm raged harder. The shape became clearer with each passing second.

It was me—the old man me.

Well, a gray, foggy version of me, dripping with blood. Its movements were slow and jagged, like a puppet controlled by strings about to snap.

"I am your past, your present, and your future," the figure growled, its voice deep and hollow.

I stumbled backward, my heart pounding like thunder in my ears.

The gray figure's lips twisted into a sneer, and its voice dropped into a groggy whisper as it reached out a hand.

"I am you."

CHAPTER 23
AN ANGEL AT THE GATEWAY

I woke in a cold sweat, scrambling upright and scraping my arm on the concrete. Just a dream—no, a nightmare.

I made my way upstairs to do the chores again, my mind still tangled in the nightmare's hold. The words circled in my head, "I am your past, your present, and your future..."

What did that mean?

Even as I scrubbed dishes and took out the trash, I couldn't shake the eerie feeling. The walk to school didn't help either. My brain replayed those words like a broken record, each repetition making my stomach twist just a little more.

"James, wait up!" a familiar voice called from behind me.

I turned just in time for Tom to crash into me, his arms wrapping around me like a vise. His face was streaked with tears.

"Tom, what's wrong?" I asked, flinching from the pain as his grip pressed into my bruises.

"I heard the Goodmans took you back," he said, his voice shaking. "Don't worry—we're going to get you out of there."

I broke free of Tom's grasp and stepped away. "I can't talk about this." Let alone be sure I could get through this day. "We'll be late if we don't get moving."

"Right. Sorry," he muttered, wiping his face.

The school hallways felt oddly unfamiliar. Nothing had changed—same chipped lockers, same faded posters hanging crookedly on the walls—yet it all felt so foreign.

First period passed without much incident. Most of the teachers still looked like they'd given up on life, their lackluster lectures blending into the background. The one exception was my history teacher. He looked completely different—like a younger, polished version of himself.

Gone was the middle-aged man with rumpled clothes and slouched posture. His hair was now neatly cut, and he looked lean and confident, his new glasses adding an air of professionalism. The only thing that hadn't changed was the ever-present coffee stain on his collar. It didn't matter if it was a new shirt; the stain was practically his trademark.

Lady Luck must've been watching out for me today because Alex was out sick. Not having to deal with him felt like a minor miracle. I didn't know how much more I could handle, and I was grateful for the reprieve.

THE DAY PASSED UNEVENTFULLY, JUST AS I'D HOPED. THE final bell rang through the halls, signaling the end of the day.

"James, who's that girl waiting for you at the gate?" a classmate asked as we left the building.

I stared at him blankly, my mind trying to place a name with his face. Then it clicked. "What do you mean, Tony?"

"The brown-haired angel by the gate," Tony said, pointing. "She said her name was Alysa."

"Alysa?" I repeated, my stomach flipping as I scanned the crowd.

Sure enough, there she was, her radiant smile standing out like a beacon.

"Hey, James! How are you?" she called, turning toward me with that one-in-a-million grin.

I shrugged. "I'm doing okay," I said, glancing away to hide the cut on my head.

Alysa's eyes narrowed, her smile fading. Before I could react, she grabbed my face and tilted it down to her level.

"I thought so," she said, her voice tinged with disappointment.

"What?" I asked, jerking back.

"They beat you again," she said softly, shaking her head as if I'd let her down. "Well, at least this will help us win the case."

"What case?" I asked, confused.

"I don't have time to explain right now," she said, rummaging in her bag and pulling out a pair of scissors. "But can I have some of your hair?"

"What?" I said, stepping back as she held the scissors up. "Why?"

"Just trust me," she said, tapping her foot impatiently.

Reluctantly, I grabbed the scissors and snipped off a chunk of hair from the back of my head where it would be less noticeable. I handed it to her, still unsure what she wanted it for.

"Thanks." Alysa beamed at me like I'd just handed her a winning lottery ticket. Then, without another word, she turned and skipped away.

I stood there, stunned. "What the hell just happened?"

CHAPTER 24

DNA

The sound of footsteps rumbled above me, sending specks of dust floating into the air. I rolled over quickly to look at the clock. I wasn't late to start chores. Derrick must have gotten up early.

Unsure of what awaited me, I went about my morning with caution. I got dressed as quickly as I could and made my way upstairs to start my chores. I caught a glimpse of Derrick out of the corner of my eye.

Drunk. He was rummaging around in the fridge. He grumbled and slammed the door shut before he left the room.

I breathed a sigh of relief and went about my morning. Jackass was probably up all night.

School was just another prison, but at least I didn't have to be on edge the entire time. I moved through the hallways like a ghost, hearing conversations but not really listening, sitting through classes but not really learning. Every second felt like it stretched longer than it should, each tick of the clock dragging me closer to the inevitable—the end of the day, where the Goodmans would be waiting.

The weight of dread I felt was insurmountable.

Between whatever Alysa's plan was, the DNA test, the hope of something changing—it felt impossibly distant. What if it wasn't enough? Maybe I should have reported the abuse sooner. But I knew deep down it wouldn't matter. Not with Pam's dad in charge of things over there. What if the test came back and nothing changes? Everything continues the way it has for the last several years? What if one day Derrick beats me into the next life?

The thought followed me as I slid into my last class of the day, my fingers gripping the desk just a little too tightly. My mind drifted all day, back to the conversation I had with Alysa about the accident.

The one that took my parents' lives.

Ever since Alysa mentioned the typo in the records, I haven't been able to stop thinking about it.

A child had died in the crash. A woman had died in the crash. A man was missing.

A man was missing.

My dad was missing.

My stomach twisted.

That wasn't a mistake, a simple typo. There was something deliberate about it. It's hard to mix up a missing child with a missing man. Right?

A mistake would be misspelling a name, mixing up a detail—not completely mistaking two dead adults and a missing child.

The thought made my head pound.

"Okay class, take out your laptops and start working on your report," the teacher announced, pulling me back to the classroom.

The fluorescent lights buzzed softly overhead as I reached into my bag and pulled out the school-issued laptop. I opened up the Word document containing my report. Then, separately, opened a web browser behind it. I pulled open the police records website and started digging through the archives.

It didn't take long to locate the collision report. Two dead. One child missing. Alysa was wrong.

Two dead.

Mom and Dad.

I scrolled down.

Cause of accident: unknown.

Then I saw it.

My heart started thumping.

The responding officer on the scene of the crash: Officer Charles Stephens.

A jolt of fear ran down my spine.

Stephens.

I read it again, my brain struggling to accept the truth. Then, I opened up another tab, pulling up the police department employee roster.

Charles Stephens was now Chief Stephens.

Pam Goodman's father.

A wave of nausea rolled through me. I sat there, staring at the screen, my breath unsteady. Pam Goodman always had power over me. The way the school never questioned her. The way she and Derrick had adopted me so easily. The way the system had always worked in their favor.

And now I knew why.

Her father was the one who responded to the crash. He had been there.

What did he cover up?

The bell rang, startling me back to reality. I grabbed my things and hurried toward the front of the school. Sure enough, Derrick's rusted sedan sat at the curb, engine squealing as it idled. I caught a glimpse of his impatient scowl as I slid into the backseat, my pulse still hammering.

Derrick said nothing at first. The silence was heavy. "You sure took your sweet time and wasted more of mine." His words were laced with venom, each syllable a poisonous injection.

I didn't answer.

I didn't know what to say. I didn't know what to think.

But this was all deeper than I could have ever imagined.

CHAPTER 25
COURT NOTICE

The Goodmans' house was its usual battleground of yelling and sarcasm. I started in on the dishes that had accumulated since I left for school this morning.

"Derrick, go get the mail!" Pam's voice screeched across the house.

"Why don't you get it yourself, *Paaaam*," Derrick yelled back, pointedly drawing out her name with mocking intonation.

"Because I don't feel like it. Now, be a gentleman for once in your life," Pam shot back. She flipped through a magazine with a dismissive wave.

"Fine!" Derrick grumbled, stomping out the door like a sulky teenager. Moments later, he returned, a stack of envelopes in hand. At the top of the pile was an official-looking letter—like something from the government or a lawyer, maybe. Pam snatched the letter, her eyes quickly scanning its contents before, in a sudden fit of frustrated anger, she violently ripped it to shreds.

I bit my tongue, avoiding the overwhelming urge to ask about the letter. The last thing I needed was to add fuel to a raging fire, ready to lash out. Instead, I kept my head down and focused on the dishes, the soap, the sponge.

"You must feel *soooo* smart," Pam sneered.

At first, I didn't realize she was addressing me, so I didn't react. But her tone sharpened. In my peripheral, I could see her turning her attention to me.

"Well, boy, your stupid little friends are taking us to court," Pam said, her lips curling into a cruel smile. "You better shape up."

Derrick, who had been sorting through the mail, perked at her words. "Pam, you're saying I get one more crack at him before the big day?"

"Yes, but leave him presentable," Pam replied, her tone ice cold as she settled back into her chair.

Derrick grinned and started cracking his knuckles. I think he thinks it makes him look tough. "Can do. You ready, boy?"

My heart sank. "What are you guys talking about? I didn't do anything!" I stammered, backing away from him.

Derrick chuckled darkly, his face twisted with amusement. "Because you ran away, other people found out about our little secret. You didn't really think we'd let that slide, did you?"

Before I could respond, his fist connected with my jaw. The impact wasn't as hard as it could have been, but my body was so worn down from years of abuse that even a weak punch was enough to send me crumpling to the floor. And, as always, one punch wasn't enough for Derrick.

The blows kept coming—fists, kicks, anything he could throw at me. I lost count after a while, my mind numbing to the pain as his relentless assault blurred into a haze of agony.

"That's enough, Derrick," she said, her tone sharp. "We need him to look presentable."

Derrick scoffed but stepped back, clearly pleased with his handiwork. Pam knelt beside me, her expression cold but calculated. She began tending to my wounds, not out of compassion but to make sure I looked decent for their court appearance. Her touch was rough, muttering the entire time. But somehow, she patched me up well enough to stop the bleeding.

After Derrick and Pam left the room, I crawled toward the torn-up letter on the floor. Ignoring the pain, I pieced it back together, smoothing the jagged edges as best I could.

April 16th

Dear Goodmans,

We were informed of your mistreatment of the young master upon his arrival. As such, we have begun the necessary preparations for his retrieval. After extensive research, we are now ready to proceed.

This letter serves as an official notice to Pam and Derrick Goodman.

If you do not surrender custody of James Shipman to us within two days, we will take legal action to resolve this matter in court.

—The Schiffs

TODAY WAS THE 17TH. TWO DAYS? THAT MEANT tomorrow would be the deadline. There was no way the Goodmans would willingly give me up, and I doubted the Schiffs expected them to.

For the first time in years, I wasn't thrown onto the cold, bare floor of the basement. Instead, I was given pillows and blankets. It was almost laughable how obvious their motives were—they needed me to heal, at least on the surface, to avoid looking suspicious in court.

Still, the special treatment felt like a minor victory, even if it was short-lived. As I lay on the surprisingly comfortable cot, my thoughts drifted away from the Goodmans and their schemes. My mind conjured an image of the manor's long driveway, golden light streaming through the trees, and the warm, welcoming smiles of Alysa and the Schiffs waiting for me at the end.

That vision was my last thought before sleep claimed me.

CHAPTER 26
TREASURE BOUND

When I opened my eyes, I was back in the cave. The Baron's Revenge floated silently in the center of the underground cavern, its dark hull glistening under the soft glow of the lamps.

The stillness was unsettling—until I remembered I still hadn't seen the rest of the house. My curiosity outweighed my unease, so I climbed the narrow staircase leading out of the cave, determined to explore.

As I wandered through the manor, it took two doors before I discovered several large chests overflowing with gold coins, sparkling gems, and ornate treasures embroidered with intricate patterns. Each room in this manor held a different trove of wealth. I pocketed coins for later, mentally categorizing what was in the manor, where the wealth was, and how I could get it out.

Eventually, I made my way outside, stepping through the grand front doors and onto a wide pathway carved into the mountainside. It wasn't an easy climb, which also meant whoever lived here would need to be strong or smart.

"If there's anyone down there, maybe I can get some answers." I paused, glancing back at the manor. "This place is strange enough. I don't want to be here when the owner comes back, so I have to move fast."

After a moment of indecision, I began the descent. The path was long and winding, but the scenery was breathtaking. The mountain was alive with lush greenery and wildflowers, and the crisp air carried salt on the wind. By the time I reached the base of the hill, the bustling sights and sounds of a thriving port town greeted me.

Colorful buildings, with bright and welcoming facades, lined the town's streets. Sailors and merchants filled the cobblestone walkways, their laughter and chatter creating a lively atmosphere.

. . .

AIMLESSLY WANDERING, I EVENTUALLY STOOD IN FRONT OF a tavern called The Sailor's Oasis. The boisterous cheers of revelers and the raucous singing of sea shanties spilled out into the street, filling the air with energy. Drawn in by the noise, I stepped inside.

The interior was just as lively as the outside. The crowd swayed and danced to the music, their voices joining the singers in an impromptu choir. I weaved through the throng, eventually finding a seat at the bar, where a young bartender greeted me with a warm smile.

"What can I get for you?" she asked, with a toothy smile and a sparkle in her eye.

"A whiskey," I said. The words left my mouth without a thought.

"It's a lively night, isn't it?" she remarked, grabbing a bottle from the shelf behind her.

"Yeah, it definitely is," I said, glancing over my shoulder at the commotion. "Hey, for a little extra, can I ask you something?"

"No need for that," she said with a grin, pouring the amber liquid into a glass and sliding it across the counter. "What do you want to know?"

"The manor on the hill—who lives there?" I asked, studying her reaction while trying to remain nonchalant.

"No one's lived there in years," the bartender said, leaning on the counter, exposing her long neck to me. "The last owner passed away about a decade ago."

"Interesting," I said, taking a small sip of the whiskey. The burn was unexpected, and I tried not to cough. "Do you think any of the folks here might be interested in signing on to a crew?"

"It's possible. There's always work needed in a town like this. Eagerness is abundant. You can use that table over there if you want to recruit," she said, pointing to an empty wooden table near the crowd.

"Thanks. But before I go, I've got two more questions," I said, turning back to her.

"Oh yeah?" She crossed her arms, waiting.

"What's your name, and do you have a night off? I'd like to invite you to dinner," I said, finishing my drink with a small smile.

Her cheeks flushed faintly, but her tone stayed light. "Hmm, okay. It's Aurora, and I'm free Tuesday night."

"Perfect. I'll see you then," I said, pushing away from the bar.

Over the next couple of hours, I recruited sailors. Each new crewmember seemed rough around the edges, but they had the confidence and experience I needed.

A few drunken blokes started causing trouble. When Aurora asked them to leave, they refused.

"Get these guys out of here!" Aurora shouted, her voice cutting through the noise.

I jumped up to help, along with a few others. Together, we dragged two unruly sailors toward the door. But just as I was about to step outside, the world spun as pain exploded across my skull. Glass shattered, and I collapsed to the ground.

Darkness swallowed me whole.

CHAPTER 27
COURT DAY

My eyes fluttered open, and reality hit me like a punch to the gut. I was still here, imprisoned in the suffocating confines of the Goodmans' house.

Dragging myself out of bed, I made my way downstairs, clinging to the faintest hope. Maybe—just maybe—the sudden kindness after receiving the notice meant some kind of change. Perhaps today, there would be a pre-made breakfast waiting or a reprieve from chores.

I shouldn't hope.

Instead, the house was a worse disaster than last night. Dirty dishes towered in the sink. Sticky floors, overflowing garbage, clothes strewn across the furniture, and the bathroom, reeking from down the hall, was characterized by the Goodmans lounging lazily in the living room.

The dishes were first. The Goodmans insisted I use the hottest water possible, and my hands burned as I scrubbed. It took nearly an hour to finish the mountain of plates, cups, and pans.

Next came the rest of the house. Vacuuming, arranging the couch, wiping tables, mopping floors, and cleaning windows were all straightforward enough. But the bathroom was another story.

The stench hit me as soon as I opened the door, sharp and overwhelming. Scrubbing the tiles, cleaning the toilet, and using harsh chemicals left me dizzy and nauseous. Sometimes, I think Derrick misses the toilet on purpose, just so I'll have to clean his mess.

After taking out the trash and tackling the laundry, I finally finished. By the time I was done, it was noon. Normally, I stayed on top of the chores to keep them manageable, but my absence had left them to pile up into an overwhelming mess.

"Pam?" I gently called from the hallway.

"What, demon child?" Her tone was sharp as a blade.

"I... um, I finished the chores," I said, keeping my distance.

"Good. Now clean yourself up. You look pitiful," she snapped, her eyes narrowing. "We will not let you go so easily. If anything, we'll work you to death first." Her lips curled into a cruel smile.

"Okay..." I muttered, retreating toward the bathroom.

The chemical stench still lingered, making my head spin. Standing in front of the mirror, I did my best to hide the bruises with cheap makeup they'd bought. It barely made a difference. I combed my hair with an old, jagged comb that scraped at my scalp, brushed my teeth with a mix of mint, water, and a sponge I found under the sink, and changed into the least tattered clothes I could find.

At least these weren't bloodstained.

"Pam," I called hesitantly from the bathroom doorway.

"What now, spawn of Satan?" she barked, her voice laced with venom.

"I'm done changing," I said, keeping my head low.

"Good. Now sit on your hands in the corner and be quiet," she ordered with a dismissive wave. "Those damn butlers aren't getting you back. Not while you're with us."

I nodded and walked to the corner, lowering

myself onto the floor and sitting on my hands. My fingers quickly went numb, but I didn't dare move.

I stared at the floor, trying to keep my thoughts from spiraling, but they came anyway. The ruling in this case will irrevocably determine not only my future but also whether or not I will have any chance of experiencing freedom, happiness, and a life free from the horrors of this nightmare.

If the Goodmans won, I'd be trapped in their clutches, forced to endure their cruelty until my body gave out. If the Schiffs succeeded, maybe—just maybe—I'd have a shot at something better.

All I could do now was wait. My hands ached while my heart clung to a hope that felt impossibly far away.

CHAPTER 28

THE PAM AND DEREK SHOW

"Pammmmmm!" Derrick bellowed, his voice cutting through the air like a rusted blade.

"What?" Pam croaked.

"Get my nice shirt!" Derrick hollered from the bathroom, his voice brimming with aggression.

"Why?" Pam shot back defiantly, her voice rising in pitch.

"So you can get off your lazy butt and work off some of that fat," Derrick snarled.

"I ain't fat," Pam snapped.

"Oh, right—I forgot. You stay skinny because you never stop chewing on those 'special snacks' of yours," Derrick said.

"Get your own damn shirt," Pam barked, grabbing the newspaper from the couch and flipping it open with a sharp crack.

Through the entire argument, I sat quietly in the corner, hands and arms now numb from sitting on them for so long. This was my life. Most kids had TV or video games. I had front-row seats to the endless reruns of *The Pam and Derrick Show*. They hurled insults at each other like they were trying to break a world record.

"Hurry up, Derrick! We're going to be late!" Pam shouted without looking up from her newspaper.

"Wait a damn minute—I'm almost done." Derrick's voice was muffled by the bathroom door.

Five minutes later, Derrick strutted out of the bathroom, chest puffed out. His idea of "dressed up" was a cheap button-up shirt and slightly less-ripped blue jeans.

"Wow, Derrick. You look better than the day I found you," Pam said, sauntering over to him like they hadn't just been tearing each other apart moments ago. "Why'd you never get dressed up for me?"

If this was his best, I could only imagine what he looked like *when she found him.*

"Thanks, Pam," Derrick said, sucking in his

stomach and standing up straighter like he thought he was impressing her.

"Of course," she said sweetly, before spinning around to face me. Her tone shifted. "Get up, demon child."

My hands were pins and needles. I pushed myself to my feet, using the wall for support.

"Let's go," Pam hissed, marching toward the door.

We piled into their rusted, two-door brown Honda CRX. One taillight was shattered, and the back right tire was nearly flat. Derrick jammed the key into the ignition and twisted it.

Click. Click. Sputter.

The car coughed and died.

"Come on, you piece of junk," Derrick growled, trying again.

Sputter. Clunk. Silence.

On the fifth try, Derrick let out a roar of frustration, stomped out of the car, and kicked the front bumper with enough force to crack the left headlight.

Somehow, when he climbed back in and turned the key again, the engine sputtered and roared to life. It sounded like someone throwing rocks into a garbage disposal.

The ride was as painful as I'd expected. The clutch squeaked with every shift, and the gears ground so loudly I could practically feel the car falling apart. The flat tire flopped with every rotation, and the suspension was so stiff it felt like every bump in the road was a punch to my battered spine.

By the time we reached the courthouse, I was lightheaded from the exhaust fumes and sore from the brutal ride.

I stumbled out of the car, taking in the massive building before me. The courthouse loomed overhead, its pristine white exterior gleaming in the sunlight. Intricately engraved pillars lined the façade, and a grand staircase led up to imposing dark oak French doors.

Inside, the elegance was more overwhelming. The walls were adorned with enormous paintings of the first eight U.S. presidents: George Washington, John Adams, Thomas Jefferson, James Madison, James Monroe, John Quincy Adams, Andrew Jackson, and Martin Van Buren. Each painting hung in perfect order, five on each side, their stern faces staring down at anyone who dared walk through.

The floor was polished quartz that shimmered under the overhead lights. In the center of the room, a long red rug with gold fringes stretched across the floor, leading directly to another set of dark oak French doors.

I followed behind Pam and Derrick as they marched toward the courtroom, my heart thudding in my chest with every step. This moment pressed down on me like a lead blanket.

This was it.

The beginning of the fight for my freedom—or the confirmation of my imprisonment.

CHAPTER 29
CASE CLOSED

The judge's gavel struck the block with a sharp *crack*, silencing the whispers in the courtroom.

"Next case," the bailiff called. "Custody hearing regarding minor James Shipmen."

Judge Hollis adjusted his glasses and glanced over the paperwork before him. His voice echoed through the room, calm but firm. "This hearing is to determine the rightful guardianship of James Shipmen. The petitioners, Mr. and Mrs. Schiff, assert that the current foster placement with the Goodmans is invalid."

Pam Goodman stood up, smoothing her skirt even though her hands trembled. "Your Honor, we've had legal custody of James through the foster system for years now."

Judge Hollis raised one eyebrow. "According to the documents submitted by the Schiffs, there is reason to believe James was placed in foster care due to a clerical error."

Pam stiffened. "And what exactly do these documents say?"

"Mrs. Goodman," the judge warned, "I suggest you keep your tone respectful in this courtroom."

Pam sat down quickly, mumbling, "Sorry, Your Honor."

The judge shuffled a few papers, then read aloud. "The Schiffs have provided a certified DNA test confirming that James is the biological child of the late Jay and Marisa Shipmen. Additionally, they've submitted a notarized guardianship directive, signed by the Shipmens before their passing, granting custody to the Schiffs—who served as the family's long-time caretakers."

He paused and looked over the rim of his glasses. "Based on this evidence, the court recognizes the legal guardianship of Mr. and Mrs. Schiff. Custody of James Shipmen will be transferred to them immediately."

Pam shot to her feet. "You can't do this! Do you even know who my father is?"

Judge Hollis didn't flinch. "I am aware that Chief Stephens is your father. His position does not influence this court. Unless you have a valid legal objection—?"

Pam opened her mouth, then closed it again. Derrick stared straight ahead, his face pale.

"Very well," the judge said briskly. "Custody is officially awarded to the Schiffs. Court is adjourned."

Crack! The gavel struck one final time, and just like that, it was over.

At that moment, a heavy weight lifted from my chest. The invisible chains that had bound me for years fell away, leaving me feeling light—free.

"You piece of trash! That fortune should be ours!" Pam shouted.

"What?" I said, puzzled.

"The manor, the money, all of it," Pam screamed. "That's the only reason we took you in. And you will give us what you owe!"

She scowled at me, then plopped back into her seat. I was so surprised and overwhelmed that my thoughts were a complete jumble—I didn't know what to think.

For the first time, I allowed myself to truly look at the Schiffs. All three of them stood together, smiling warmly at me, as if welcoming me into the life I'd only ever dreamed of. Alysa's smile, in particular, radiated pure joy—a sight so reassuring it filled me with hope for the future.

But then something changed.

Her expression shifted, her smile fading into worry. My heart sank as I felt a sharp pressure on my shoulder.

Thud! WHACK!

The room erupted into chaos. My vision blurred, and I struggled to make sense of what was happening.

Ba-dum—Ba-dum—Ba-dum—

The sound of my heartbeat pounded in my ears as my knees buckled. I hit the ground hard, but the pain barely registered.

Ba-dum—Ba-dum—

Shadows danced across my vision. The world faded in and out, and the noise around me became a distant hum. I tried to reach out, but my arms felt heavy—unresponsive.

Ba-dum—Ba-dum—

The last thing I saw was Alysa's terrified face, her mouth moving in silent words I couldn't hear.

Then everything went dark.

CHAPTER 30
CONFUSION

Beep... beep... beep.

The steady rhythm of a heart monitor cut through the haze clouding my mind, each beep pulling me closer to the surface of consciousness.

"James? James? Wake up, James! Please—" a sweet voice pleaded, distant but persistently.

"Give him some space, honey. He'll wake up soon," came a deeper, more formal voice, calm and steady.

My eyelids felt glued shut. Slowly I managed to force them open a peep. Blinding white light spilled into my vision. I blinked back the light and slowly, blurry shapes took form. Alysa's tear-streaked face hovered above me, her wide eyes full of worry.

"What... happened? My head feel like a truck hit it?" I rasped.

"Just stay still, James. The paramedics are checking you," Alysa said, her voice trembled.

"Paramedics?" I croaked, trying to sit up, but a sharp pain shot through my head, pinning me back. Two paramedics leaned over me—one holding a blood-stained cloth, the other preparing a needle and thread.

"Why are there paramedics?" I asked again.

"Do you really not remember?" Alysa asked.

"What do you mean? We just won? What happened?" The pounding in my head grew more intense with every syllable spoken.

"James," Alysa said, her grip on my hand tightening slightly as she spoke, "Please calm down. We won the case, but Derrick—he snapped. After the judge's decision, he grabbed your shoulder, threw you into the wall, and you hit your head pretty hard. You've been out cold." Her voice faltered. "Immediately afterward, they took Derrick into custody, and after a cop got a look at you they arrested Pam too. Someone called for paramedics immediately."

Her words took a moment to sink in.

"Wait... what?" I managed, my voice weak and disbelieving.

"The paramedics said you'll be fine, but you need to let them finish their checks," Alysa said, her tone softer now. "They're going to transport you to the hospital. Once the doctors have given you the all-clear, we can finally go home."

CHAPTER 31
THE RETURN HOME

The soft groan of the hospital door opening pulled me from restlessness. My eyes fluttered open, adjusting to the sharp contrast between fluorescent light and the golden streaks of late afternoon sunlight streaming through the windows.

"James? Are you ready to go?" Alysa's voice, warm and full of relief, reached me from the doorway.

I blinked a few times and sat up on the edge of the hospital bed. My body ached, and my head still throbbed faintly, but the sight of Alysa's smile made the pain feel far away.

"Yeah, I think so," I said, my voice raspier than I expected.

She stepped inside, her footsteps echoing lightly in the quiet room, and handed me a fresh set of clothes—much nicer than the hospital gown I was wearing. As I changed, I caught my reflection in the small mirror on the wall. My face was bruised, but there was a glimmer of hope in my eyes I hadn't seen in a long time.

Once I was dressed, Sebastian wheeled me into the hallway, with Alysa following close behind. The door creaked as it shut behind us. The sound felt oddly final, like the closing of a chapter in a book.

The wide, sterile hallway smelled faintly of disinfectant, and the rhythmic squeak of the wheelchair's wheels echoed as we headed toward the exit. A nurse held the door open, and as I was wheeled outside, a soft breeze greeted me, carrying the scent of freshly cut grass.

For the first time in as long as I could remember, I felt free. It was like the weight of my past had finally lifted, leaving me light enough to float on the breeze.

Parked at the curb was a sleek, gloss-black Mercedes, its polished surface reflecting the sunlight like a mirror. Sebastian offered a hand to help me stand and slide into the car. The plush leather seats were a stark contrast to the hard, cramped rides I was used to. The quiet hum of the engine was surreal.

The ride was smooth, the world outside the window passing in a blur of vibrant colors. The trees along the road danced in the wind, their green leaves shimmering in the sunlight. We climbed the hill toward the manor and wound our way through the long driveway to the grand gates, their intricate ship engraving glowing in the afternoon light. As they opened, the manor came into view—more magnificent than I remembered.

Sebastian parked near the grand fountain, and Alysa practically bounced out of the car, her excitement contagious. I followed her into the manor, a place that seemingly overnight had become home.

This was my home.

This was all mine.

"James, if you want to change out of those bloody clothes, there are new ones waiting for your arrival," Sebastian said. "But the doctor said you shouldn't shower just yet. You're welcome to use a washcloth, but please avoid your head. I'll need to help you with that bit."

"Okay. Thank you," I said.

Home... I was home.

Instead of climbing the left staircase, Sebastian

insisted we use the service elevator. While chattering enthusiastically about the building's unique architectural elements, he informed me the elevator had been installed in the 1950s. As he guided me to my room, it dawned on me for the first time that Sebastian had been genuinely frightened on my behalf. The realization filled me with a strange mix of emotions.

My room was just as I'd left it—clean, elegant, and inviting. The closet was full of clothes I'd never had a chance to wear before, and somehow, even more things I was confident hadn't been there last time. The wardrobe ranged from formal suits to cozy sweats. I chose sweatpants and a clean T-shirt.

Sebastian helped me with the shirt. I'd needed eight stitches in my head. The doctor also said that at some point, I'd broken two ribs—and he'd seen several old fractures that had already healed. There was inflammation... somewhere. I honestly can't even remember where. They're going to monitor me.

From home.

I still can't get over it.

After changing, Sebastian and I headed back downstairs.

We entered the dining room, and I stopped in my tracks. A feast worthy of royalty covered the long, elegant wooden table. Every resident of the manor was there, smiling and clapping.

"Welcome home, James," Sebastian said, raising a glass in a toast.

Looking around at the people who truly cared about me, I felt a lump rise in my throat.

For the first time in my life, I wasn't just surviving—I was home.

CHAPTER 32
PLANNING

The gentle click of the latch, the creak of the hinges, and the final thunk of the study's oak doors closing behind me felt heavier than it should have—like the decisions I was about to make carried the weight of generations. I turned to face Sebastian, who stood just outside, always ready, always waiting.

"Sebastian, do you remember what I asked you —like a lifetime ago?" I said, approaching him as he oversaw the bustling work of the manor's staff.

"Good morning, James. Hmm, I'm not sure I recall. Remind me?" he asked, adjusting his vest.

"It was about *The Baron's Revenge*," I said, pointing toward the manor's basement. "I asked how many people it would take to crew her."

"Ah, yes," Sebastian said, his expression brightening as he nodded. "You'd need at least eighty crew members to man her properly."

"How many people do we currently have on the estate?" I asked, already calculating how short we were.

"After some recent hiring, we're at twenty-three," Sebastian said.

I sighed, rubbing the back of my neck. "That's not nearly enough. Is there a sustainable way to crew *The Baron's Revenge*—something that can both maintain her and make her useful?"

Sebastian's eyes gleamed with sudden inspiration. "We could offer tours of the ship itself, invite visitors to see her grandeur. Additionally, we could hire a larger crew and send her out for afternoon voyages—perhaps even some... let's say, *lucrative* expeditions—while she's in port."

"You mean piracy?" I asked, raising an eyebrow.

Sebastian chuckled softly. "If we're being direct —yes."

I considered it for a moment, then nodded. "Could you make that work?"

"Why not? It's what built all of this," he said, pulling out the small notebook he always carried and jotting down notes. "But I think the tour idea could really work. An immersive experience like that could be quite lucrative. I'll look into it and get back to you."

"You're the best, Sebastian," I said with a grin.

He gave me a rare smile in return. "Have you eaten breakfast yet, James?"

"No, not yet. I'm heading to the kitchen now."

"Good. Go on, then," he said, waving me off as he strode away to begin preparations.

The kitchen greeted me with the irresistible aroma of a full breakfast platter—fluffy eggs, golden biscuits, sweet jam, and perfectly cooked sausage. I ate slowly, savoring every bite. Eating scraps felt like a lifetime ago, and I was determined to enjoy every bit of this breakfast before heading to the back deck to think over the day's plans.

The breeze was gentle, and the sun peeked through the trees. In the distance, I spotted Alysa standing in the field, her white dress flowing in the wind, her hair catching the sunlight.

I'd promised to spend time with her today. The thought made me smile as I made my way toward her.

Later that morning, I stood behind my desk, flipping through the documents Sebastian had left for me. The study was a grand room with large windows overlooking the manor's sprawling gardens. Books, artifacts, and heirlooms from the Shipmen family's long history filled the shelves lining the walls.

"Sebastian, can you step into the study for a moment?" I called out.

"Yes, James?" he said, entering through the open double doors.

"I've been reviewing the documents you prepared about *The Baron's Revenge*," I said, pulling the stack of papers from a desk drawer.

"And?" Sebastian asked, his posture relaxing slightly.

"I've made my decision. We'll hire a larger crew, host tours to bring in revenue, and send her out on missions—because she'd be wasted otherwise. Will you be able to arrange that?" I asked, handing the papers back to him.

"Of course," Sebastian said, though his voice trailed off.

I narrowed my eyes. "Is something wrong, Sebastian?"

"Did you happen to see the other folder I placed on your desk this morning?" he asked, a hint of guilt in his voice.

I rifled through the stack of papers and pulled out a slim folder labeled *James*. "What's this?"

Sebastian straightened his vest before replying. "It's tradition. The previous heads of the family were all trained in martial arts, swordplay, and firearms. I took the liberty of hiring tutors for you. Your lessons begin tomorrow."

I stared at him, surprised. "You went behind my back?"

"I apologize," he said, bowing slightly. "It *is* tradition, but I should have checked with you first."

I shook my head with a small laugh. "It's fine. You could've told me. Sword fighting, huh? That could be fun."

CHAPTER 33
SWORD PLAY

"You're late," Sebastian remarked from across the courtyard, arms folded as he watched me approach.

"I—" I started to protest, but thought better of it. He wasn't wrong. I was late.

Sebastian nodded toward the man standing beside him. "James, this is your first instructor, Mr. Parker. His expertise lies in the art of swordsmanship. He'll provide you with comprehensive training in wielding a blade, honing your skills, and mastering the art of combat."

Mr. Parker gave a curt nod. He was lean and tall, his stance rigid—yet when he moved, his body flowed like water. His sharp gaze studied me, measuring.

"I don't waste time," Mr. Parker said, gesturing toward a rack of practice swords. "Pick one."

I grabbed a blade—the weight heavier than I expected. Parker walked over and corrected my grip with a swift tap against my knuckles.

"Dominant hand at the pommel to support the balance. Off-hand here, guiding the motion," he instructed. "Now, follow my lead."

He moved through a series of swings, each motion precise, like an intricate dance. I mimicked him, but my movements felt sluggish and clumsy in comparison.

"Feel the blade, James," he said, watching me intently.

I furrowed my brow. "What does that even mean?"

He exhaled, shaking his head. "A sword isn't just a tool. It's an extension of your body. You control the weight, the momentum—just as you control your own limbs."

I tried again, adjusting my stance and focusing on the weight distribution. The blade cut through the air in a smoother arc this time, but as I followed through, my balance wavered. I stumbled backward.

"Footwork, James." Parker crouched and picked up a stone, holding it at arm's length. "If I keep my feet planted and extend my arm, the weight strains my muscles. But if I shift my stance, the weight redistributes—making it easier to control."

I nodded, gripping the sword again. I planted my foot, adjusted my weight, and swung. This time, the movement felt cleaner, the blade gliding through the air effortlessly.

Parker's eyes flickered with approval. "Better. Now, block."

Before I could react, his blade came down. Pure instinct made me raise my sword, deflecting his strike just as I sidestepped.

Parker lowered his weapon. "Not bad. You'll need practice—but you're not hopeless." He turned on his heel, already walking away. "Practice. Tomorrow, I won't warn you before I strike."

I smirked, exhaling as I wiped the sweat from my brow. "Thanks, Mr. Parker."

The next couple of weeks fell into a rhythm. I woke, ate, trained, ate, trained, slept—then repeated it all over again. Every day, I got better. Every day, my body moved a little faster, a little stronger, a little more in sync with the blade.

CHAPTER 34
STRAIGHT SHOOTER

After the first week of sword fighting, it was time to increase my lesson load. Distant gunfire cracked through the crisp morning air, followed by the faint rustle of birds scattering from the treetops.

"Master James," Sebastian called from across the training grounds, standing beside a tall, wiry man with a rifle slung over his shoulder. "This is Mr. Carter. He will oversee your firearms training."

Mr. Carter moved toward me with an eerie smoothness, his steps silent despite the gravel crunching beneath his boots. His presence was unsettling—not intimidating. He moved with calculated steps, always aware of the surrounding space.

Without a word, he extended a pistol, grip first.

"First lesson is safety," Mr. Carter said, his voice low but firm. "Never put your finger on the trigger until you're ready to fire. Got it?"

I nodded, adjusting my grip and resting my index finger alongside the barrel like I had seen in movies.

"Good. Next, stance." Carter motioned for me to widen my feet. "Right foot back, left foot forward, knees slightly bent. Keep your weight balanced—your hips should face the target."

A row of practice dummies stood at the far end of the courtyard. I lined up my stance as instructed, but before I could take my shot—

The sudden gunshot made me flinch. A small puff of smoke drifted from the end of Carter's rifle as the bullet ripped cleanly through the center of a dummy's head.

"Focus," Carter muttered, lowering his weapon. He wasn't even looking at me—his gaze stayed locked on the target, unfazed.

I swallowed hard and turned back to my own pistol.

"The weapon is an extension of yourself," he continued. "Every movement, every breath—it all has to be deliberate. No haste. No panic. The gun is an instrument of control, not chaos."

I lined up the sights, inhaling deeply. The world around me blurred, my heartbeat syncing with my steadying hands. My finger hovered over the trigger —light, delicate, yet holding immense power.

Bang!

The shot scattering a flock of birds from the nearby trees. I lowered the pistol, eyes locked on the target. My bullet had struck near the upper torso a bit off-center—not terrible for a first try.

Carter gave a nod of approval. "Not bad. You've got the basics."

He reached behind him, pulling a rifle from his shoulder and handing it to me. "Now, let's step it up. Same rules apply, but this time, your left hand supports the forestock. Keep the butt of the rifle snug against your shoulder."

I adjusted my grip, glancing at him for confirmation. "Like this?"

"Exactly. Now, line up your sights and take your shot. No rush—let the right moment come to you."

Peering down the rifle's iron sights, I steadied my breath. The slight sway of the barrel wavered over the target, but as my breathing slowed, the movement lessened. My world shrank to just me and the target.

I squeezed the trigger.

Bang!

The rifle kicked against my shoulder, but the bullet struck dead center.

A small smirk tugged at the corner of Carter's lips. "You're a natural, kid. Keep practicing, and you'll be an expert before you know it."

CHAPTER 35
DINING WITH THE CHEFS

Alysa stood beneath the courtyard archway, holding a woven basket against her hip. Not who I expected to meet—but a pleasant surprise all the same.

"Come on, James! It's lunchtime. Eat with me," Alysa called, waving me over.

I grabbed a towel, wiped the sweat from my forehead, and picked up my things before heading her way.

"Finally. You're so slow," she teased, spinning on her heel as I caught up.

"Mind if we stop by the office first? I want to drop off my stuff," I said, admiring how her hair caught the light.

"I guess," she said, though her voice held a slight

hesitation. Her bright green eyes flickered with something I couldn't place.

I slowed my pace. "Something wrong?"

She let out a small sigh. "It's just... I don't really know how to put this, but I worry you're over-working yourself. You're always training, always in the office. You don't have to push yourself so hard, you know?"

That caught me off guard. I scrambled for a response.

"I—I'm sorry?" It was all I could come up with.

"Sorry? Why?"

"I don't know. For making you worry, I guess?" I offered a small smile. "Once I get a handle on every-thing, I'll hire someone to help."

She studied me for a second, then exhaled, her shoulders relaxing. "Okay, fine. But you'd better not overdo it."

I wasn't great at reading people, but I could tell she felt at least a little better.

"I've been thinking a lot since your court date," Alysa said.

"Oh?" I asked.

"What if the chief of police and the Goodmans set up your parents? Killed them on purpose to get your fortune? There were a lot of inaccuracies in that report," she said.

"It won't bring them back," I said plainly. "I'm here with you. With all of you. This is where I belong. Going after the Goodmans—or even the chief of police—won't bring my parents back. Besides, we don't have the evidence. I've decided to make peace with it."

Alysa smiled, but it felt... somehow forced. We continued through the manor in silence.

We dropped off my things in the office before heading to the dining room, where the table was laid out with a feast—shrimp scampi, crab cakes, pan-seared scallops, and freshly baked garlic bread, each dish still steaming with heat. The rich, mouthwatering aroma alone made my stomach clench with hunger.

"I asked the chefs to prepare some of their favorites for lunch, so everything would be ready by the time we got back," Alysa said, taking a seat.

I hesitated before sitting down next to her. "This all looks amazing... but there's so much."

"We could invite the chefs to join us. They haven't taken their lunch break yet, and I'm sure they'd love to eat with you," she suggested. "You may not realize it, but they admire you a lot."

I glanced at her. "You really think they'd want to?"

"Yes! Of course." She tilted her head. "Want me to go get them?"

I shook my head. "No, I'd rather thank them myself."

She smiled as I stood and extended my hand to her. Carefully, she took it, and together, we made our way to the kitchen.

The closer we got, the richer the aroma became —garlic, butter, fresh herbs. Steam curled through the air, and the sounds of sizzling oil and clanking pans filled the hallway. As I pushed open the dual swinging doors, the kitchen fell momentarily silent.

The chefs turned, eyes widening slightly. For a second, no one spoke.

Then, as if out of habit, they lined up, as though expecting some sort of formal command.

"There's no need for that," I said, waving a hand. A few exchanged uncertain glances before relaxing slightly.

"I just wanted to thank you all for this incredible meal. You've made so much, and it all looks amazing. I'd hate for any of it to go to waste, so... would you all join us?"

They stood quietly for a moment before their faces lit up.

The dining hall, which had felt far too large and quiet before, soon filled with laughter and conversation. The table, once a display of wealth and tradition, now overflowed with warmth and life.

Surrounded by the kitchen staff and Alysa, I listened to stories. We shared a meal, and I realized something—this, right here, felt more like home than anything ever had.

CHAPTER 36
A DAY OUT

Alysa practically skipped into the room, excitement radiating off her as she dropped a basket onto my desk with a soft thud.

"James! I have an amazing idea—and my dad's already on board," she said, grinning from ear to ear.

I barely had time to react before she grabbed my arm, practically pulling me out of my chair.

"What are you talking about?" I asked, stumbling slightly as I tried to keep up.

"Let's go sailing!" she announced, shoving a bundle of clothes into my arms.

I blinked down at the pile—a loose white shirt with undone laces around the collar, a deep blue family vest embroidered with the golden jackdaw crest, a thick black belt, and a pair of worn tan jeans with more pockets than I could count. When I glanced back at her, I noticed she had changed too. Instead of her usual dress, she wore baggy cargo jeans, a nearly identical white shirt, and a vest like mine—only without the family crest.

"Come on, change already!" she said, shifting from foot to foot with barely-contained energy.

With a tired sigh, I pulled the shirt over my head and dressed quickly, barely buckling my belt before Alysa grabbed my wrist and tugged me down the stairs.

We passed the main hall, turned into the library, and came to an abrupt stop in front of the old bookshelf. Without hesitation, Alysa reached for one of the leather-bound tomes and gave it a sharp tug. The shelf groaned, then slid back, revealing the dimly lit passage that led down to the littoral cave where the ships were docked.

"Wait... there's no way we can sail *The Baron's Revenge*," I said, hesitating at the top of the stairs.

She smirked. "We're not sailing *The Baron's Revenge*. We're taking out *The Sun's Shadow*."

She pulled me forward again, and as we rounded the bottom of the stairs, I finally saw it—a sleek black-and-gold, forty-five-foot beauty nestled behind *The Baron's Revenge*. Smaller, sure, but still impressive. My eyes landed on the pirate flag hanging from the mast. At first glance, it looked like a standard skull and crossbones—until I noticed the golden family crest tucked into the right eye socket.

"Wait... you *have* sailed before, right?" Alysa's voice snapped me out of my thoughts.

I hesitated, then cleared my throat. "I may have exaggerated the first time you asked. I don't know much, but I've been reading up on it."

"Well, what *do* you remember?" she asked, her grin never fading.

"I kind of remember how to tie knots and raise the masts... but that's about it," I admitted, scratching the back of my head.

She laughed. "Then we'll just practice around the shore today. I packed lunch and water so we can take a break out there."

"That sounds amazing." I climbed aboard, settling beneath the mainmast.

"Alright," Alysa called from the helm. "Unfurl the jib sails—the ones at the front," she pointed.

I grabbed the rope and slowly loosened it, letting the sails drop. As they caught the wind, *The Sun's Shadow* gave a small lurch forward, gliding through the dark waters of the cave.

Alysa carefully navigated us through the rock archway at the entrance, sunlight spilling through in sharp contrast to the cave's shadows. Below us, the water was a deep but clear blue. Fish darted between rocks and ribbons of seaweed.

The moment we broke into open waters, she called, "Alright, unfurl the fore staysail and the fore-sail—the ones on the tallest mast."

I nodded and released the sails, watching as they billowed out, catching the wind instantly. The boat picked up speed, slicing through the waves. I turned back to check for more instructions, but she wasn't looking at me.

Her smile was wider than the horizon, her eyes reflecting the ocean itself.

"Alysa," I called.

She laughed nervously. "Come back here and let down the mainsail. Then we'll *really* start moving."

Climbing over ropes and ducking under beams, I made my way to the mainsail. As I loosened the rigging, the massive canvas unfurled, catching the wind with a powerful *snap*. The ship surged forward, cutting through the water with exhilarating speed.

Salt sprayed into the air, a cool mist against my sun-warmed skin. The ropes bit into my hands, but I didn't care. The broken waves behind us shimmered like scattered diamonds. I had never felt so free.

We sailed for hours, losing track of time, guided only by the shifting position of the sun. The ocean stretched endlessly around us, the wind carrying us forward with effortless grace. It wasn't until the sky turned soft with evening hues that we finally turned back toward the manor.

By the time we docked, my hands were raw from the ropes, my skin sun-kissed and salty, and my entire body ached with exhaustion.

I slept like the glorious dead that night.

CHAPTER 37
RECRUITMENT BEGINS

"Master James, are you awake?" Sebastian's voice carried through the door.

I groaned, rolling over. "Five more minutes, Sebastian."

Pain shot through my body—my arms felt like lead, my legs ached, and my hands tingled from the strain of training and sailing the day before. Even my face burned, probably from too much time in the sun.

"It's already ten, Master James. Are you all right in there? I'm coming in."

The door creaked open, and Sebastian stepped inside, a folder tucked under his arm. Without a word, he walked to the heavy curtains and yanked them open, flooding the room with blinding sunlight. My head pounded instantly, and I groaned again, forcing myself to sit up.

"What's so important that you had to wake me up?" I muttered, rubbing my eyes.

Sebastian turned, already laying out my formal clothes. "Do you remember requesting that I find a crew for *The Baron's Revenge*?"

I blinked, trying to focus. "Yeah... wait, don't tell me—"

"I gathered them here. They're waiting outside for you."

I shot upright, ignoring the protests from every sore muscle in my body. "They're here? Like, right now?"

Sebastian nodded, smoothing out my vest. "It would be unwise to keep them waiting much longer."

"Right, right—" I jumped out of bed and hurried to get dressed. "Thanks, Sebastian."

"Of course, Master James."

By the time I rushed down the stairs, still buttoning my vest, Alysa was already waiting at the bottom with a piece of toast in her hand.

"Here, eat this," she said, shoving it toward me.

I took it without slowing down, holding it between my teeth as I cinched my tie. The grand front doors loomed ahead. With one deep breath, I threw them open.

Before me stood a massive crowd—fifty men strong, all gathered in the courtyard. A wave of anticipation rolled through them as they turned toward me.

Sebastian discreetly handed me a few cue cards. I barely glanced at them before stepping forward.

"Thank you for answering my call, adventurers!" I called out, letting my voice carry across the courtyard. The murmurs stilled. Heads turned. "I offer you a rare opportunity—one few will ever receive. I command a true galleon, *The Baron's Revenge*, a ship built for exploration, strength, and legacy. And today, I ask: who among you will sail under my command?"

Silence stretched.

"I understand your hesitation," I continued. "So let me be clear. You'll be given fair accommodations, food, and water. You'll be paid in coin. And if you have families, they'll be provided housing—free of charge. Pledge your loyalty to my house, and we'll care for you like our own."

Still quiet. I took a breath and pushed more energy into my voice.

"The housing will take time to prepare," I admitted. "But while we work on that, those waiting will be compensated." I raised my voice higher. "So tell me—do you seek adventure?"

The silence cracked.

"Yes!"

"Do you seek thrill?"

"Yeah!"

"Do you want glory, riches, and the freedom of the sea?" I tossed the cue cards aside, heart pounding.

The crowd erupted into cheers.

"Then join me!" I shouted. "On both sides of the manor, you'll find registration tables. List your name, the position you seek, and how many in your household need housing. We'll be in contact soon."

The crowd surged toward the tables.

I turned toward Sebastian. "How many stations are set up?"

"Five on each side, with rotating teams," he replied without hesitation.

I exhaled. "That should be enough... I hope."

"Shall I return to the office to oversee the paperwork?"

"Yes, and—" I paused, fatigue catching up again. "I need a bit of rest. I'll check in later."

Sebastian gave a small nod. "Of course. If you need me, I'll be in your office."

With that, he strode off into the manor. I barely made it to the sitting room before collapsing onto the couch.

I must've dozed off, because when I woke again, the sun had shifted. The manor was quiet.

Rubbing my eyes, I pushed myself up. The registration was handled—but a bigger question gnawed at me: how was I supposed to *sustain* all these people?

With a sigh, I headed for Sebastian's office, hoping he was still there.

When I pushed the door open, the room was empty.

"Okay," I muttered. "Guess I'll just write it down."

I grabbed a piece of parchment, dipped a pen in ink, and started writing.

Sebastian,
I didn't rest well. My mind kept racing about how to sustain so many people.

The best idea I've come up with is to start the tours as soon as possible.

But instead of simple tours, what if we run it like a luxury cruise?

Charge a premium for the authenticity of the ship. Let the base fare cover food, crew wages, and operating costs.

We should also consider building more ships for different purposes.

Expanding into property rental might also be smart—buy more land, develop housing.

We'll need a proper dock built near the estate, separate from the manor, to handle operations.

A seaside café could be profitable too.

There are a lot of possibilities—but I trust you to decide what's in our best interest.

Let's finalize the plan soon so I can actually sleep again.

—James

AFTER SIGNING MY NAME, I FOLDED THE PARCHMENT AND walked upstairs, sliding the note under Sebastian's door.

With a yawn, I turned toward my room.

"I'm still exhausted. I think I'll call it a day early."

And with that, I shut the door behind me.

CHAPTER 38

FINAL PLANS AND THE JACKDAW'S NEST

"**M**aster James, this isn't where you should rest," Sebastian's voice came from across the study.

I blinked, adjusting to the light streaming through the window. My cheek was pressed against the wooden desk, a few scattered documents slightly crumpled beneath me.

"Oh... Sebastian. I've been meaning to talk to you," I muttered sleepily, pushing myself up. My neck ached from the awkward angle, and my arms felt heavy.

"You shouldn't fall asleep at your desk," Sebastian said with a sigh, picking up the papers I'd left in a pile the night before. "But I assume this is about the note you left under my door?"

"Yeah," I said, rubbing my temples. "We need to go over everything—the funding for the crew, the dock, the cruise, and the restaurant idea."

Sebastian took a seat across from me, setting a thick file onto the desk. "I read through your proposal. Expanding to a luxury cruise model is an excellent idea, and it will generate enough income to sustain the crew. The seaside restaurant, though, will take a bit more investment before it turns a profit."

"I figured," I said, flipping through my notes. "But I think if we make it fully immersive—pirate décor, servers in costume—it could stand out. If we turn it into a tourist attraction, it might fund itself."

Sebastian nodded. "Yes, and we'll need to move the dock to a separate location, as you suggested."

I reached for the map and unrolled it between us. "How much property do we actually own around the estate?"

Sebastian pulled a pencil from his vest and traced a rough perimeter along the map—a sprawling section of coastline, including several nearby islands.

"Approximately this much, Master James."

I studied the map, following the curves of the

shoreline with my eyes. Then I spotted it—a small inlet, the perfect size for our project.

"There," I pointed. "We don't need to build it all at once. We start with the cruise, using *The Baron's Revenge* for voyages when it's not running tours. Once we're financially stable, we build the restaurant."

Sebastian examined the map, then leaned back with a rare smile. "Genius."

I looked up at him, surprised. "What?"

"The entire plan—it's brilliant. If executed correctly, it will bring in a fortune." He clasped his hands together, his expression warm. "Your parents would be proud."

A lump rose in my throat at the mention of my parents. I don't remember them, but knowing I was honoring their name made my chest tighten.

"You really think so?" I asked quietly.

Sebastian nodded. "Without a doubt."

He stood and retrieved something from a shelf, wrapped in a deep blue cloth. Gently, he placed it on the desk and unwrapped it—revealing a stunning one-handed longsword.

My breath caught. The blade was black as night, its edge gleaming like distant stars. The hilt bore the Shipmen family insignia, engraved in intricate gold.

"This is one of your family's heirlooms," Sebastian said, offering it to me.

I ran my fingers over the engravings, feeling the weight of its history. "This is... incredible."

Sebastian handed me the sword's belt, his gaze steady. "You've earned it, Master James."

I swallowed hard. "Thank you, Sebastian. For everything."

He gave a slight bow, pride in his expression. "Always, Master James."

Then he straightened and gathered the papers we'd discussed. "Shall I commence preparations for the dock?"

"Yes," I said, fastening the belt at my waist. "Let's get started."

Sebastian turned to leave but paused at the door. "Ah, I almost forgot. Alysa is waiting for you by *The Sun's Shadow*. She said she wanted to show you something."

"Alright, I'll head down now," I said, adjusting the sword at my side before following him out.

The cavern was cool and dim as I made my way past *The Baron's Revenge* toward *The Sun's Shadow*. Alysa stood at the helm, tapping her foot impatiently.

"What took you so long?" she called out.

"Sebastian and I were finalizing some plans," I said, hopping onto the deck.

She rolled her eyes playfully. "You're always talking about work. Let's go do something fun."

I raised an eyebrow. "What exactly do you have in mind?"

Alysa grinned. "We're sailing to Jackdaw's Nest to watch the sunset."

That actually sounded... nice.

"Alright, alright," I said, moving to unfurl the sails. "Let's get going."

The ship glided smoothly through the water, picking up speed as the sails caught the wind. The sea air was crisp, the scent of salt and adventure filling my lungs.

For a while, neither of us spoke. We just sailed, the world quiet except for the rhythmic crash of waves and the occasional creak of the ship.

The sun was already beginning its descent by the time we reached the shore.

Alysa jumped onto the sand and motioned for me to follow. "Come on! I know the perfect spot."

I secured the ship and hurried after her, rounding a bend until we reached a massive boulder nestled between two palm trees. The view stretched out endlessly, the sun sinking toward the horizon in a breathtaking display of color.

I exhaled, taking in the sight. "Wow."

Alysa sat down, patting the spot next to her. "Right?"

I joined her, resting my arms on my knees. The air was warm, the sound of the waves steady and calming.

For a while, we just sat there, watching the sky shift from gold to deep orange, then soft violet. It was the most at peace I'd felt in a long time.

Alysa leaned back slightly, turning toward me. "See? I told you this would be better than paperwork."

I chuckled. "Yeah, yeah. You were right."

She grinned triumphantly before settling into a comfortable silence.

This moment—sitting on a quiet beach, feeling the last warmth of the sun on my skin—was something I wanted to hold on to.

For the first time in a while, I wasn't thinking about responsibilities or expectations.

Just this.

Just now.

CHAPTER 39
DARK HALL OF THE ANCESTORS

The sky churned above me, storm clouds rolling like waves—thick and dark, swallowing the horizon in shadow. I stood knee-deep in the ocean, yet I wasn't drowning. The water lapped at my body like a gentle embrace, cradling me as if it were part of me.

When I stepped onto the shore, my clothes were dry, untouched by the sea. The sand beneath my feet rippled unnaturally, shifting like the surface of a disturbed pond. Before me, Jackdaw's Nest loomed —but it wasn't as I remembered. The island was cloaked in an eerie, colorless twilight. No sun, no moon—just the dim glow of stormlight filtering through fast-moving clouds. Trees swayed violently, as if caught in a gale, yet I felt no wind.

"What is going on?" I murmured, confusion pressing heavy against my chest. "Why do I keep having these dreams?"

"Welcome, Captain Jack Shipman."

A voice like rolling thunder shattered the silence, its presence vibrating through the very fabric of the island.

I turned sharply, pulse hammering. "Who are you?"

"I have guided you through your family's history."

The words crashed over me like waves on rock—powerful and resonant. The air turned electric, charged with something ancient.

"Come out and face me!" I called, scanning the landscape, my eyes darting across the storm-twisted sky.

"This is not our last meeting," the voice boomed. "I will fade into history once more—until your children, or your children's children, or *their* children awaken my presence. Then, I will tell the full story."

I froze. "The... full story?"

"You never thought of your past, your present, and your future. But now—now you are curious. And I took advantage of that."

A surge of unease twisted in my gut. The voice

was right. I had been too focused on surviving, on escaping, on moving forward. I'd never stopped to look back.

"But why now?" I asked, stepping closer to the heart of the island.

"Because time is short."

The words rang with a finality that sent a chill through my bones. The storm above twisted, clouds spiraling into a dark vortex. The wind howled—though I still felt nothing on my skin.

"Captain Shipman, your legacy will be kept. Your stories will live on. But for now, our time is at an end."

"Wait—what do you mean?!" I shouted, panic creeping into my voice.

No answer.

The sky cracked open like a wound. Lightning rained down in rapid succession, striking the earth with white-hot fury. The air sizzled, alive with raw energy—until—

BOOM!

A single, precise bolt struck me where I stood.

Darkness.

The silence was deafening.

I couldn't move. Couldn't see. Couldn't breathe.

I was weightless, yet somehow heavy—like stone sinking to the ocean floor. My mind raced, clawing for understanding.

Where am I? What just happened? Who... am I?

A sharp ache formed behind my eyes, spreading like a crack in fragile glass.

Then—**falling**.

The sensation overtook me, sudden and unstoppable, as if the world had vanished beneath my feet. My stomach lurched. The void twisted around me until—

I stopped.

I hung in nothingness, my body suspended midair. Every breath, every heartbeat felt magnified. My senses sharpened.

Then—out of the darkness—*something* appeared.

At first, it was only a faint shimmer, like ripples in still water. But as I drifted toward it, the image became clearer.

It was me. The real me. **Fifteen-year-old James Shipman**.

Lying exactly where I had fallen asleep on Jackdaw's Nest, next to Alysa. Frozen in time.

But as I drew closer, the scene shifted. The trees

swayed naturally. The waves lapped at the shore. The sky softened, calm again.

I braced myself as I crashed through the vision—

CRACK!

Like shattering glass, the world split apart—

—and I was flung back into my body.

CHAPTER 40
GRANDFATHER

The soft shuffle of waves against the shore and the gentle rustling of palm leaves overhead stirred me from sleep. My body felt heavy, weighed down by exhaustion—but something else clung to my mind. Something unseen, like a fading whisper.

"James? James, are you okay?"

Alysa's voice cut through the haze, tight with worry.

I blinked, adjusting to the dimming light of the evening sky. "Yeah? What's up?"

She hesitated, biting her lip. "You were stirring in your sleep, like you were fighting something. And then—" She trailed off, wringing her hands.

"What did I say?" I asked, leaning closer.

Alysa's gaze dropped. "I know it's probably nothing, just a dream, but..." she sighed, "you said, *Darkness*."

I stilled.

Then it hit me—all at once.

The memories flooded in, clear and vivid. Not just my own, but those of my great-grandfather. My grandfather.

I saw him—Jaxon Shipman—as a child, perched on his father's lap, listening to stories. Captain Jack Shipman's deep, rumbling voice echoed through the memory, telling tales of the sea, of battles fought and won, of treasures unearthed and enemies bested.

"The world belongs to those who dare to take it, Jaxon," Jack said, running a hand through his son's unruly hair. "But taking isn't enough. You must build something with what you claim. Something that lasts."

The words vibrated in my bones, carrying me further back—to the beginning of it all.

The scent of wood and salt. A pub, dimly lit, alive with laughter and drunken shanties. Aurora stood behind the bar, her dark hair loose, her green eyes sharp as she poured a drink for a burly sailor.

A flash—Jack and Aurora rebuilding the manor

together. Jack restoring crumbling stone walls, Aurora sketching plans by candlelight. They turned it into something more than a fortress. They made it a *home*.

They brought in traders, craftspeople, old crewmates searching for a place to retire. They didn't just build wealth—they built a legacy.

Jaxon was born. And suddenly, the love shifted. It was no longer about conquest.

It was about *creation*.

A torrent of memories surged through me like a storm, shifting and reforming, relentless and full of life.

Now Jaxon stood at the bow of a sleek, fast-moving ship, his coat snapping in the wind. The sea stretched endlessly before him—wild, untamed.

Then—gunfire.

A rival ship loomed beside them. Pirates spilled over the rails. Steel and smoke. Salt and blood. Jaxon fought fiercely—until he spotted *her*.

A woman.

Maya.

She wasn't just fighting—she was *winning*. Every strike was calculated. Every move spoke of experience. She had the kind of presence that made men pause before challenging her.

Jaxon didn't know it then, but in that moment, he had just met his future wife.

The memories surged again. Maya and Jaxon on the cliffs behind the manor, the wind in her hair.

"You miss it, don't you?" he whispered, arms wrapped around her.

"Some nights, yeah," she replied.

"Then let's make a new adventure," he said. "Together."

And they did.

They expanded the manor. Recruited people. Built trade. Forged alliances. Jaxon led with strategy. Maya with strength and diplomacy. Together, they turned the Shipman name into something untouchable.

Then Jaxon held his own son—Jay Shipman. *My* father.

The weight of it all crushed me. Hope. History. Generations that came before me, who fought not just to survive, but to build something that *mattered*. Not just for themselves—but for everyone who followed.

A lump rose in my throat. Grief? Rage? Pride?

I didn't know.

But I knew this:

I would not let the Shipman legacy end with me.

I blinked, returning to the present. Alysa was staring at me, confused.

"I'm sorry," I started, but before I could finish, she grabbed my shoulders.

"Stop apologizing!" she snapped, her voice shaking. "Whenever I worry about you, you say sorry—like you're some kind of burden. But you're not! I *want* to be here, James. I *want* you to let me in. So from now on, instead of saying sorry—say *thank you*."

Her green eyes locked onto mine, unwavering.

I swallowed hard. Took a breath. "Sorr—" I caught myself. "Thank you."

Alysa's frown softened into a smile. "That's better."

I thought about telling her everything—the visions, the memories—but before I could say a word—

Hssssss...

The wind shifted. A slithering sound curled past my ears, like a whispering snake.

"Jamesss Ssshipmen."

A chill stabbed down my spine.

A figure stepped forward from the shadows,

cloaked in a tattered black overcoat. His hood was pulled low, his face swallowed by darkness. He was tall. Too tall. His limbs stretched unnaturally long, like shadows drawn out by a dying sun.

Alysa stiffened beside me. This time, she saw it too.

I shot to my feet, my hand flying to the hilt of my sword. "Who are you?" I demanded, voice sharp.

Alysa moved behind me. I whispered, "Get back. Now."

The figure tilted its head.

"Why sssuch jumpinesss, young Ssshipmen?" His laughter slithered into my brain like smoke, oily and taunting.

I gritted my teeth. "I won't ask again—what do you want?"

A low, rasping chuckle. "Nnnothing... yet. I am merely a messengerrr."

Alysa's body tensed. I didn't lower my blade.

"A messenger?" I asked.

"Yesss. I bring word... Your fatherrr... isss *alive*."

The world froze.

The sword in my hand felt weightless. My breath caught.

My father?

Alive?

That wasn't possible. He'd been gone for years. He and my mother had died in that car crash—hadn't they?

"What?" My guard faltered.

"James, look out!" Alysa shouted.

The figure moved—no, *vanished*—lunging toward us in a blur of black ash.

I swung instinctively, but before my sword could connect—

Whoosh.

He disintegrated, his form scattering like burning embers in the wind.

Silence.

My legs buckled. I sank to the ground, a thunderous pulse in my ears. My mind reeled, clawing for answers.

"James!" Alysa dropped beside me, gripping my shoulders. "Are you okay? What just happened?"

I stared ahead, stunned. My voice came out in a whisper.

"My father... is alive."

ABOUT THE AUTHOR

Skyler Anhalt is a 15-year-old high school freshman who enjoys writing, soccer, cars, music, and exploring local coffee shops. When he's not busy with school or extracurriculars, you can find him working out at the gym, practicing on the soccer field, or diving into creative projects.

A true car enthusiast, Skyler has a special passion for JDM vehicles. Some of his all-time favorites include the Nissan Skyline GTR (R31–R35), Mazda RX-7, Toyota Supra MK4, Honda NSX, Mitsubishi Evo X, and the Nissan Silvia S13. His love for vehicles doesn't stop at cars—he's also fascinated by motorcycles, especially the Kawasaki Ninja H2R, BMW S1000RR, and Suzuki Hayabusa. Though he knows some of his dream rides aren't beginner-friendly, he looks forward to building an impressive collection someday.

When it's time to unwind, Skyler enjoys relaxing with music, playing video games, or tinkering in the woodshop. His favorite animal is the cat—even if they don't always return the love—and his favorite color is purple, a theme proudly reflected in many of the things he owns.

Acknowledgments

Dad, thank you for pushing me to start writing this book. I wouldn't have even thought to pick up writing again without your encouragement.

Mom, thank you for supporting me through this process. There were times when I wasn't sure about what I was writing, but you always listened and helped me work through it.

To my grandparents—your excitement for this book kept me going. From the moment I said I wanted to write a novel, you've been eager to read it, and that motivation meant everything to me.

Miranda, when I first told you about the book, I wasn't sure how you'd react. But the moment you heard the idea, you were ecstatic, and that boosted my confidence more than you know.

ALSO FROM RAINBOW QUARTZ PUBLISHING

MIRANDA LEVI

From A Youth A Fountain Did Flow

The Sea Withdrew

A Tear In Time

Mo(ther) Na(ture)

In Orion's Hands

ISLA WATTS

A Fairy Bad Day

Surprise! You're a Vampire

Gorgeous, Gorgeous, Gorgons

Mork The Handsome Orc

Adopted By Werewolves

Bite Me If You Can

That's The Spirit!

LORELAI HAMILTON

Encyclopedia of Divination

Encyclopedia of Cryptids

Encyclopedia of Faeries

Tarot Tales and Magic Spells

Teenage Tarot

Arcane In Verse

The Eclectic Witch's Grimoire

Teenage Witch's Grimoire

Find Your Bliss

Tarot Reflection Journal

Tarot Refection Journal Coloring The Tarot

Dream Journal

JACKSON ANHALT

From The 911 Files